SAVANNAH LEE

MIDNIGHT MATED

Midnight Mated

Clover Pack

Book One

Savannah Lee

Savannah Lee

Midnight Mated: Clover Pack Book 1

Copyright © 2023 by Savannah Lee

All rights reserved.

No part of this book may be reproduced, stored in a retrieval system, or transmitted in any form or by any means, without the prior permission in writing of the publisher, nor be otherwise circulated in any form of binding or cover than that in which it is published and without a similar condition, including this condition, being imposed on the subsequent purchaser. All characters in this publication other than those clearly in the public domain are fictitious, and any resemblance to real persons, living or dead, is purely coincidental.

The story, all names, characters, and incidents portrayed in this production are fictitious. No identification with actual persons (living or deceased), places, buildings, and products is intended or should be inferred.

Inquiries: savannahleenovels@gmail.com

Cover Design by JV Arts

Editing by Wildfire Editing

Formatting by Unalive Promotions

Interior Art by Saralyn Everhart with Crafted Chaos

*For all my girls who have ever been wronged by a Chad. Or a Brad.
And don't forget Josh.
Or literally any douche.
Turn the page, this one's for you.*

ignore the burning sensation that meant tears were on the horizon. I'd rather die than let him see me cry.

"Move," I demanded, proud that my voice didn't shake. We love the small victories here.

"We can work this out. She doesn't mean anything to me!" I ignored my slight sense of satisfaction at the indignant squeal from my bed. I didn't do second chances. I'd been burned too many times by too many people to let that be a thing anymore.

"Move," I repeated, infusing my voice with as much malice as possible. It wasn't hard.

Chad wasn't the brightest bulb, but he proved just how dim he was when he decided to touch me. My skin crawled when he lunged at my arm, vice-gripping it so hard I knew there'd be a bruise in the morning. I didn't hesitate, my hand balled into a fist as I pulled it back, punching him straight in the nose. I relished the crunch under my fist, a pained groan escaping him.

The thud as his ass hit the ground was incredibly satisfying.

"Go fuck yourself, Chad," I said as I stepped over his legs and towards the front door. The walls shook from the force as I slammed it shut behind me.

He didn't follow.

My hands shook as I pulled out my keys and unlocked the door to my ancient Ford Focus in the storming rain outside. I had lovingly nicknamed her Stupid Bitch, or SB for short. I'd bought her five years ago, already well past her prime, but I'd needed a place to live after my foster parents kicked me out the day I'd turned eighteen. She was all I could afford, and I thanked the stars every day that she still started.

No sooner had I slid into the driver's seat before the floodgates exploded, and I let my sorrows out right there in the parking lot. I wasn't crying so much for Chad; things had been fizzling in our two-year relationship, although I never thought he'd cheat on me.

No, I cried for myself. I didn't have anyone to go to. I never knew my family, left on the front stoop of a fire station when I was only a few days old. The only friend I'd ever managed to keep around was SB. During the day, I slung coffee to overcaffeinated office workers alongside a bunch of high school kids.

I was in this alone.

Now twenty-three, Chad had been the first guy I'd trusted enough to live with. Worst decision I'd ever made. I stared at my reflection in my car's mirror, my red-rimmed chocolate-brown eyes judging me from the other side. *Get it together.*

I looked around my car, despair setting in as I realized I'd be sleeping in the already too-small backseat. Unfortunately, not a new experience for me. Chad had been out of work for a few weeks, and I'd been covering his share of bills for the past few months, my meager savings almost completely drained. And how did he repay me? By sticking his dick where it didn't belong.

It's not like it's the first time, Rowan—home sweet home.

I racked my brain for where I could park; I didn't want to sit out here in the parking lot like a loser where he might eventually come out and see me. How pathetic would that be? I felt sorry for myself for a few minutes before finally deciding on the beach. The beach always made everything better, and it was only a few hours away. I had no reason to stay here anymore. I could find a new job anywhere.

I began driving, the miles flying by as my internal pity party continued. A few hours later, I was on the outskirts of a small town called Clover, the rain continuing to hammer down on my windshield in a steady downpour. Dense, lush forest lined the simple two-lane road leading towards town, a blur of rich green and mahogany.

I wrapped my anger around myself like a cloak as I drove, tired of feeling sorry for myself. I would never see Chad again, not after that. Everything was replaceable except my dignity. I had moved in a few months ago when his roommate moved out, so luckily, I wasn't on a lease I'd have to worry about.

The cell phone I had thrown on the passenger seat lit up like a Christmas tree, the incessant blaring of the ringtone pulling me

3

out of my thoughts. I picked it up, careful to keep one eye on the road as I checked the caller ID. Chad's smiling face stared back at me, his baby blue eyes mocking me as they buzzed. I hit decline.

The phone rang two more times before the text messages started rolling in, and I couldn't help but look. At first, they were apologetic, begging for my forgiveness. It didn't take him long to turn mean, calling me names and berating me for leaving the way I did. After he'd called me a bitch for the third time, I unlocked it to reply, my temper getting the better of me.

I was too slow to react as a blur of brownish red dashed across the path of my car. I jerked the wheel hard, my cell phone flying out of my hand as I tried to avoid hitting the animal that had darted out in front of me, but it was too late. A thud sounded as I clipped it, my car reeling away with unnatural force. I screamed as my car flipped over and over, sliding and skidding through the rain, completely helpless. When the car came to a final stop, I was dangling upside down, my long stick-straight blonde hair piling on what used to be the car's roof, littered with bits of glass.

Did an animal just . . . hit me?

I took stock of my body for injuries. There would definitely be some cuts and bruises, but I was mostly okay. Thank god for seatbelts; SB had saved the day again. I was pleased when I hit the latch on mine and was rewarded with a release, dropping into an ungraceful pile on the roof-turned-floor. I gingerly pulled myself over the dash, the windshield now completely gone. I winced as bits of glass pierced my skin on the way out.

Now in the rain, I looked around for the animal I had hit but could neither see nor hear much over the roar of the storm. A flash of lightning lit up the night sky, and I looked down, a giant shadow reflecting behind my own. I spun around, fear rushing through me.

I had only a split second before the first bite landed on my flesh. A cry escaped me as a searing pain erupted in my hip. My body was lifted off the ground and flung, and I sobbed as something in my leg snapped as I collided with a tree lining the road. I squinted through the rain, whimpering as a hulking figure on all fours stalked toward me.

My attacker looked like a wolf, except for its massive size. Reddish-brown fur covered it from head to toe, and I could barely make out the piercing color of its golden eyes as the rain poured down. A low rumble sounded, and it took me a few seconds to realize it was a growl; the noise so alien to my human ears. Through bared teeth, I could see its pearly whites glinting at me in the dark.

"Please, no," I begged, ignoring the little voice in my head that said arguing with a wild animal was stupid. I outstretched my hands in front of me in a placating gesture. I tried to scoot away, but my leg protested from underneath me, bent at an unnatural angle. A loud hiss escaped me as I moved, the pain almost too much to bear.

The beast continued its advance, its golden eyes boring holes into mine. I tried moving back again but was halted by the excruciating pain in my hip and leg. My hands were wet from the blood pooling beneath me. In a few seconds, the wolf would be close enough to attack.

Holy crap, I was going to die.

It lunged, its teeth digging into my ankle this time, and I screamed as I felt the bones give way under its monstrous teeth. It pulled, dragging me across the gravel by my leg, and for a brief second, I thought I might lose the limb altogether. Darkness danced at the edge of my vision, threatening to pull me under.

As I struggled to stay conscious, an electric hum thrummed to life inside my body, intensifying until I thought I might burst. Is this what dying felt like?

The creature paused its torturous dragging, walking up my body until we were face to face. I held my breath, not daring to move as it cocked its head to one side, regarding me. If I didn't know any better, I'd think it was confused by something. It breathed deeply, snout almost touching my neck as it inhaled my scent. It sneezed, giving its head a slight shake, splatters of my blood mixing with the rain as it flung away from the beast. It bared its teeth at me again, a fierce growl ripping from its throat, and I knew it would kill me this time.

Anger ignited inside me, the hellhole that had been my life for the past few hours rising to the surface. The electricity inside me intensified, energy brimming just under the surface. I wasn't ready to die yet.

I lashed out with my hands, intending to punch it in the nose and scare it away. A look of shock coursed through us both as my fist connected, a bright spark of lightning erupting between us. The beast was blasted off its feet, landing on the other side of the road with a pained whimper.

Exhaustion and blood loss settled deep in my soul, and I barely clung to consciousness. As the beast returned to its feet, a shout sounded from the trees. It looked between me and the tree line before shaking its head clear and bolting off in the other direction. It moved faster than any wolf I had ever seen before.

A steady sound of feet thudded as someone ran up to my side, my vision fading as I felt my body floating away, numb to the pain. The last thing I saw before the darkness took me was a pair of flashing green eyes.

Chapter Two

I stood on the precipice of a cliff, wind whipping through my hair with the force of a tornado. The howl of the wind was so loud I'm not sure I would have been able to hear myself talk. I looked to the ground below, the steep drop sure to end the life of anyone who dared to jump. I took a step back, not ready to take that plunge.

Rowan.

I whipped around, searching through the gusts for the cause of the whisper. The voice was familiar and yet completely alien.

A figure solidified a few feet in front of me, a plain ebony cloak draped over them from head to toe. They faced away from me, unmoving.

I tried to call out, gasping for air as the wind stole the words from me, my throat straining to make a noise where none would come.

Instinctively I knew I had to see who was under the cloak. I reached my hand out, approaching with as much courage as I could muster as I fought to stand my ground against the wind. I was determined to see this through.

I struggled against the pressure, and after what felt like ages, I was mere inches away from the figure. I launched forward, gripping their shoulder firmly as I rotated them around.

A horrifying screech cut through the roar of the wind. The figure was faceless, with only smooth skin where features should have been. There was no mouth, but I knew the screech had come from this creature.

I stood frozen, my heart thundering in my chest as I took in the horrific thing before me. The wind intensified, and I couldn't help but sway with it as it rushed around me, struggling to keep my eyes open against the whirlwind.

A deafening shriek was my only warning as the figure charged forward, arms circling around me as we collided, forcing me backward.

Helpless, my feet lost all traction, and together, we launched off the cliff and into the depths below.

The arguing is what woke me up, the last remnants of my dream fading away as if it had never happened.

"You can't just leave her here and run, Cal," a frustrated male voice said.

Was he talking about me?

I kept my eyes firmly closed, not wanting to tip off that I was awake. I had no idea where I was or who these guys were, and who knows what they wanted to do with me when I woke up.

"How is that going to look?" The voice was low and smooth, speaking in a hushed tone. Trying not to wake me, I realized.

"This is your problem now," the one named Cal said, his voice deeper, more rugged. He spoke with a slight tinge of accent that I recognized only because I'd heard it from Gerard Butler first. That was the kind of voice I wanted to read me a bedtime story at night. Naked.

"You know I didn't do this...Alpha," he added, spitting the last word out like a curse.

"Callan," the first male commanded, and I felt a hot flush of power cascade over my skin, my heart thundered in my chest. I felt the insane urge to obey even though I had no command to follow. Still, after a few seconds, the desire to comply faded, leaving only the burn of the heat on my skin.

Cold laughter broke the hold, the power dispersing as quickly as it had come. I jumped as I heard the unmistakable crash of bodies against the wall.

"You should know better than to use your power on me, Wolfe. Do not make that mistake again." Even with my eyes closed, I felt the promise of blood in that statement. A new wash of power trickled over me, but this one had a colder, darker energy instead of the hot flush of the first one. It wrapped around my skin like a frigid caress, but it was oddly comforting. Almost familiar.

There was a strained silence before the thud of footsteps, and a loud slam as one of them left the room. After an exhausted sigh, I realized I was alone with the one called Wolfe.

"I know you're awake."

I jumped in surprise before sheepishly opening my eyes and pushing myself into a sitting position. I sat on a small bed in the middle of a larger room that looked like a makeshift hospital. I shivered and realized I still wore the same clothing I'd left my apartment in, damp from the rain and ripped from the...

I scrunched my eyes in confusion, unsure of what had happened. I remembered Chad and the smug look on that bitch's face when she'd seen me. Comforting anger filled me at the thought.

I strained to remember what had happened after, and a memory trickled back to me. The rain poured and the grating sound of the tires screeching as I slammed on SB's brakes, the car flipping over. My poor SB. I'd crawled out and...nothing. I had no idea what had happened, and now I was here.

Wherever this was.

Trying not to panic, I focused my eyes on the only other

person there, an impossibly tall hulk of a man. Wolfe's eyes were already on me, observing me. He had to have been at least seven feet tall with shaggy brown hair, his eyes so light they almost looked grey. I sized him up, pretty sure I'd die if I tried to fight my way out. I was scrappy, but even I had my limits. And I drew the line at a man two feet taller than me. I would have to talk my way out of here. We watched each other warily, waiting for someone to make the first move.

I tensed, ready for anything. For all I knew, he was a crazy hermit cannibal who had brought me to his secret lair. He didn't look like a psycho, but you never really know.

"I'm not going to hurt you," said the potential ax murderer. He offered me a dazzling smile that I would bet usually worked for him, but I wasn't going to fall at his feet so easily.

"Where am I?" I demanded, not wasting any time trying to be nice. Nice got women in trouble.

"You're in the heart of the Clover Forest. This is my home, along with my family." He ran a hand through his unruly locks, leaving them even more disheveled than before. "You were in a car crash last night. We found you on the side of the road."

I frowned, wracking my brain, trying to remember anything past crawling out from the wreckage. Wolfe watched me, eyes searching my face.

"What do you remember?" He spoke gently, with genuine concern in his words.

I eyed him suspiciously. Could I trust him? Maybe he was just a good Samaritan, helping me recover from the accident. If he wanted me dead, he could have easily killed me while I was passed out. I wasn't restrained, but I wasn't fool enough to think I could just walk out of here at my leisure. There was more to the story, and I was determined to figure out what.

I closed my eyes, willing my brain to connect the dots.

"I remember crashing. There was ... a wolf? Just standing there in the middle of the road, and I had to swerve." I closed my eyes, a sharp bite of pain lancing through my head as I forced it to work in overdrive. "It bit me!"

The memory of the savage attack had me reaching for my hip and ankle, and I was shocked to see they were completely intact. The only mark on my body was a small bruise near my hip where I had been bitten, but as I watched, the bruise faded gradually. At the rate it was going, it'd be healed within the next few minutes.

"What is happening to me?" I gasped, my shocked stare still trained on my hip. Maybe I was still dreaming. Or maybe Chad had pushed me over the edge into a psychotic break, and now I was in the loony bin. My breathing sped up, bordering on hyperventilation, as I thought of the unnatural creature that had attacked me—definitely a psychotic break.

Wolfe stepped toward me, and I skidded backward until I hit the edge of the couch.

"Don't touch me," I growled, panic taking hold.

Wolfe froze where he stood, and I felt the burning energy from before filter back over me. Soon my heart rate steadied, my breathing leveled out, and my thoughts stopped racing. Was he casting a spell on me or something? I felt the urge to lay down for a nap, but I fought against it, willing my eyes to stay open and focusing them on the man in front of me. My body reacted to the adrenaline coursing through me, my heart rate speeding up again.

He met my eyes with a shocked expression, but I didn't have time to dwell on that before the door to the room barged open. A beautiful long-legged goddess of a woman sauntered in, her long dark hair flowing behind her.

"Wolfe, what are you doing in here? I heard your call." Her voice was a lilting melody of notes; I could have listened to it all day.

"I want to leave," I demanded, not giving him a chance to respond. I wasn't sure where I'd go, but it sure as shit had to be better than being stuck in this place where injuries healed on their own.

"She's fighting me," he said after a moment. He exchanged a knowing look with the girl before returning to me. "You are not trapped here; you can leave if you choose. But I think you'll want to stick around after hearing what we have to say. For your own good."

I shot up, pushing gingerly to stand on my feet. I had no gaping wounds, but I was pretty sore. He didn't have to tell me twice. I was gone. I could deal with all this weirdness on my own.

"Of course, your car is completely totaled," he added, and I could have sworn I saw a slight smirk in the set of his mouth. I stopped in my tracks, a trickle of despair worming around my heart at the thought of SB. My only loyal friend.

"I can walk," I said flatly, pushing the sadness at losing my trusty sidekick to the locked box of feelings I kept inside. I could mourn my losses later. Or never.

"We're 23 miles from the highway," he said, and I was sure I saw the smirk this time.

"Then call me a cab," I huffed. I'd steal a car if I had to if it meant I didn't have to stay here.

"I'll help you out on one condition," he said, holding one long slim finger up. His grey-green eyes sparkled; he was getting a kick out of this. If I had met him at a bar and not in a strange room in the middle of the woods against my will, I might have thought he was cute, but right now, I could only think about rearranging his face.

"You let Lily give you a tour." He nodded to the woman on his right. "And this evening, you have dinner with me. If you still want to go home, I'll even give you a car to keep."

I snorted a laugh.

"Yeah right, buddy. No offense, but I'm not doing anything with you. I've seen too many true crime documentaries to fall for that crap. I'll take my chances walking." I moved around him towards the door, ready to fight if needed, but Lily stepped out of my way without hesitation. It seemed they would not physically try to force me to stay.

"Don't you want to know what attacked you? And why your injuries healed so quickly?"

For the second time, I stopped. Of course, I wanted to know.

"If you stay for dinner, I'll answer your questions. Full transparency."

I thought for a moment. What could I lose if I stayed here? Well, my life, for one. These people could very well be about to murder me. Maybe they were human traffickers, planning to ship me off to the highest bidder. I shivered at the thought.

I had nothing left to my name, my car was wrecked, and my backpack was nowhere to be seen. All I had were the clothes on my back. A car and an exit plan were a very sweet offer indeed ... if he was telling the truth.

More than that, though, I did have questions. So many questions. The animal that had attacked me looked like a wolf, but way bigger than any natural wolf I'd ever heard of. Why had I been attacked? And why had I survived? And the most important question of all, how was my body healing itself?

My need for answers outweighed my instinct for self-preservation. If they wanted to hurt me, they would have already. At least, that's what I told myself as I made what could be the biggest mistake of my life.

Taking a steadying breath, I rotated around to meet his eyes.

"You'll answer every single question I ask? And a working car to leave in after?"

His smile turned into a full-blown grin, a sparkle in his grey eyes.

He knew he had me.

Chapter Three

Lily wasted no time showing me around. She was bubbly and kind, just like I imagined she would be. It would be hard not to like her, but I could try. The last thing I wanted to do was get attached; I was leaving the first second I could.

I followed along as she led me out of the infirmary and into the bright sheen of the sun, a beautiful fall day.

"This is where we all live," she said, gesturing outside to the clearing area she had brought me to. We stood in a huge grassy field where a playground and sandbox stood empty. It struck me as strange that no one was playing when it was such a nice day outside.

"Where are the children?" I blurted out.

"There are no children that live here," she said softly, walking off in the opposite direction, shutting down the conversation completely.

Small cottages dotted the outside of the clearing in all directions, with one row backed by a much larger mansion at the very end. The other side of the circle was lined with buildings of varying shapes and sizes; I assumed recreational activities. It all looked normal. Everything was made from the same rich mahogany wood as the forest surrounding us. Stands for torches were periodically placed around the clearing. This was a community that liked to live off the land.

"There are a lot of empty houses, but we hope one day we can fill them." She beamed, clearly in love with her home. Not at all like a serial killer, and I started to relax a little. I wondered what it was like to be proud of where you came from.

"Who lives in there?" I asked, gesturing to the mansion at the back. She smiled at me, excited about my interest. I tried to hold her gaze with mine, but she cut her glance to the side after a few seconds.

"That's where Wolfe lives."

"He's the leader?" It made sense. He was the one bargaining with me for my freedom. And what had that guy in the infirmary said earlier? "Is he an Alpha?"

Maybe she would answer my questions too.

She gave me a sly look as we walked on, steering me towards the area with the more recreational buildings. "He is. To both of your questions."

"What does that mean?"

"It means he protects us. We are all family, and we protect each other. He's here to ensure we uphold that. He'll tell you more about it tonight." The finality in her tone told me I'd be getting no more from her on the topic. Irritation lanced through me at the secretiveness of it all. Why was everything such a mystery?

We stood in front of the extra buildings as she pointed them out to me individually. There was a mess hall, gymnasium, meeting hall, and the infirmary we had come from earlier. People of all shapes and sizes milled about, shooting us the occasional strange look but otherwise going on about their day. Many greeted Lily with a smile or a small hello as we walked by.

"You're probably starving; let's stop in the mess hall, then I'll show you to your house."

"My house? I don't need a house. I'm not staying."

She only smiled and ushered me into the small building on the right, the mess hall. My stomach immediately growled as my nose was assaulted with mouthwatering aromas. I don't think I'd ever smelled anything so good. My mouth watered just thinking about what it could possibly be emanating from.

The clock on the wall told me it was just past eleven in the morning. A little early for lunch and too late for breakfast, we were practically the only people in there. Only one other person sat at one of the far tables in the corner, her blonde hair in a high ponytail, facing away from us.

Lily handed me a tray as we got up to the counter. A nice-looking elderly man waved to Lily from behind a plastic partition before returning to his task of mopping the kitchen floor. The food was served buffet style, and I didn't hesitate to start grabbing. Roast beef, mashed potatoes, steamed vegetables, and dinner rolls piled on my plate high. I was small, but I couldn't remember the last time I had eaten and was starving.

I looked down the row of the buffet, realizing there was still a whole other section I had yet to go to. Turkey legs, chicken of all sorts, steaks, and hot dogs filled the bins, and I looked at them with sorrow, realizing I hadn't left enough room on my plate.

"Why so much meat?"

"We need a lot of protein," she said with a shrug, her hair whipping over her shoulder as she walked off toward the other person in the room. Did forest people need to eat more than normal people? Still trying to understand, I followed.

"Hey Evie, mind if we sit? I'm showing her around today." The girl was startled but recovered quickly.

"Sure," she said with a smile. Sliding into the seat across from her, I saw she looked a lot like me but a few years younger. Long blonde hair, big brown eyes. Chronically pale skin. We could have been sisters.

"Hi," I said, returning her smile. I wasn't sure I could trust these people, but she was just a kid. "I'm Rowan."

"Rowan," she repeated, bobbing her head like she was

committing it to memory. I started shoveling food into my mouth, now completely ravenous. When I stopped to breathe, I realized both girls were staring at me with wide eyes. I gave a sheepish grin, and Evie giggled softly under her breath.

"Rowan is new here," Lily chimed in. "Evie is also new; she's only been with us a few months." This piqued my interest.

"How'd you end up here?" I asked her, trying to ease into the fact-finding mission. I locked eyes with her, a sliver of satisfaction going through me when she looked down a few seconds later. Lily placed her hand on Evie's, cutting off whatever reply she was about to give me.

"She doesn't know yet," Lily said gently, patting Evie's hand before removing it. Evie smiled apologetically, and I wondered what she'd almost let slip.

"Doesn't know what?" I looked between them, my guard snapping firmly back in place. I knew there was something weird going on here. I pushed harder, not taking their silence for an answer. "Why won't you just answer my questions?"

"It's not my place to tell you," Lily said, not meeting my eyes. "Wolfe will tell you everything you need to know when you see him tonight."

I slammed a hand down on the table, not caring when they both jumped. Patience was a skill I sorely lacked. "Just tell me now! Why is everything such a secret here?"

Evie hesitated, looking between us before she turned to me, a fierce defiance in her eyes.

"We are not human, Rowan." I'm pretty sure my eyes bugged out of my head. I probably could have reached up and squished them back into their sockets.

"Evie!" Lily warned, but Evie paid her no mind as she held my stare.

"We're shifters."

"What. . .," I trailed off, not understanding.

"We can turn into animals. During the full moon and at will." Lily sighed at Evie's admission, slouching back in her chair while shooting the other girl a dirty look. I stared at them for a moment before the laughter I tried to stifle bubbled up and out, a slightly hysterical edge to it.

"So, this is the loony bin. Got it. I don't think I can stay for dinner." I moved to get out of my seat and get as far away from these crazy people as possible, and Lily reached up, gripping my arm firmly.

"I can show you," she said, and I paused, my curiosity getting the better of me.

When she stood up and ripped the pretty sundress she had been wearing right over her head in one swift move, I thought I might have had a heart attack. Underneath, she was completely naked, her body just as glorious as the rest of her. I fixed my eyes firmly on a spot above her head, but she only laughed at my discomfort.

"We see each other naked all the time. If we don't shift naked, our clothes get ripped. You'll get used to it." I ignored her comment, knowing full well I did not intend to stick around regardless of what she was about to do.

I kept my eyes exactly where they were until I heard the sounds of bones crunching and snapping, eerily similar to the noise I had heard when the monster bit my ankle. A few seconds later there was only silence and I looked down. I gasped, stumbling back a few steps and tripping over my feet to land on my ass. I should have run, but I could only sit frozen as fear coursed through me.

It was the beast that attacked me.

Chapter Four

Instead of lunging at me to rip my throat out as I had expected, the wolf sat in front of me with her head on her paws, wearing a patient expression. Or at least the most patient a fearsome wolf could look. Evie reached down and patted her head, and the wolf lifted her head and panted in what I could have sworn looked like a smile. Familiar brown eyes trained back on me, a gentle whine escaping her.

The more I studied her, the more I realized this couldn't have been my attacker, and I relaxed slightly. This was Lily. She was a much smaller wolf, her fur coat as silky and dark as her human hair. She had a stark, white-shaped star pattern that wove through the fur on her hide. The beast that had attacked me was much larger and not nearly as dark—more of a reddish-brown hue. I focused on bringing my breathing back to normal.

With my terror quelled, the fact that I had just seen a person transform into an animal had my mind spinning. There was no way that could be possible, but here she was, sitting right in front of me.

Holy. Freaking. Crap.

Evie offered a hand to help me up, and I took it gratefully.

"Sorry," I said. "I thought she was the animal that had attacked me last night."

Wolf-Lily gave me a pitying look before she started to shift back, and I held her dress up to help cover her. She gave me an appreciative smile.

A million more questions plagued me at the realization that they were not, in fact, crazy people. Just people that shifted into animals at will. Nope, nothing crazy here.

"So...everyone here can do that? You all turn into wolves?"

"Not exactly," she answered, adjusting her dress into its correct place. "There are all types of animals. Big and small, predatory and domestic. In this pack, we mostly have forest-dwelling animals. Wolves, birds, bears, those kinds of things. But there's really no limit on what types of animal shifters exist worldwide."

My mind spun, question after question spinning through my mind. "Wha. . .How...?" I tried and failed to formulate any coherent sentence but my brain was still stuck on the worldwide portion of this revelation.

"Take a deep breath," Lily cautioned. "It's a lot to take in, I know." Evie nodded emphatically, and I remembered she must have gone through this not too long ago. I observed her in a new light, trying to figure out what kind of animal she would turn into.

"Shifting is genetic," Lily started as we sat back down at the table. I eagerly listened, my curiosity burning a hole in my chest. It seemed Lily had given up all pretense of not answering my questions, and I was ready for more answers. "You can get it from either parent, and only one needs to be a shifter. Generally speaking, you take on the animal of your parent; however, that is not always the case. Recessive genes happen. I once met a child in India whose parents were both tigers, but he turned out to be an elephant! The situation was tense, to say the least."

Elephants and tigers? The possibilities seemed endless.

"Are there hybrid shifters? If two different animals have a child?" I finally asked, taking a few moments to decide which question to lead with. It would be cool to be able to turn into multiple animals.

"No. We only take on the gene of one animal, no exceptions." I nodded like that made sense, even though nothing about this made any sense.

"Can shifters heal faster than normal people?" It was my most burning question since I'd woken up and realized the wounds I had sustained in the attack had miraculously healed on their own.

"We can," Lily answered cautiously. "Assuming the damage isn't too bad. We can be killed."

"How do you know if you're a shifter?" There was a reason they wanted to keep me here, and a part of me wondered if it was because of this. I'd seen my wounds healing with my own eyes. I didn't feel like someone who could turn into an animal, but I also couldn't deny what I had seen.

"Not until the first shift, which happens when a shifter turns seventeen," Evie said, practically bouncing in her seat with her excitement as she spoke.

I ignored the cut of disappointment I felt at her words. At twenty-three, I was far past the age of being able to shift. There had to be another explanation for how I had healed so quickly.

"Evie here is seventeen. Shifted for the first time a few months ago." Lily beamed at the teenager, her fondness for the girl obvious.

"I'm an eagle," Evie's chest swelled with pride. "Wolfe says I have the largest wingspan of any eagle on the west coast!"

I tried to imagine little Evie shifting into a giant majestic bird, but I couldn't make the visual work. Physical size didn't have much to do with what animal a person became, it seemed.

"Are your parents eagles too?" I asked.

"I don't know my parents," Evie said softly as her face fell, and I immediately regretted my question. "I'm adopted. The first time I shifted, they panicked and kicked me out."

"Once the first shift happens, Alphas can scent out shifters if they aren't part of a pack yet. Wolfe found her in a homeless shelter in Clover."

I looked at Evie, giving her a reassuring smile. "I understand that more than you'd think. I'm glad you made it here."

And I meant it. I'd been searching for a place I belonged my entire life, and it warmed my heart that Evie had found hers.

"Was the wolf that attacked me a shifter?" I asked finally. I tried to remember the attack, trying to recall the image of the beast. My head twinged, and I winced as I blinked my eyes against the sharp pain.

"You good?" Lily asked, brows pinched together in concern.

"Just a little headache," I told her, a fake smile plastered on my face. I knew I should tell her about the pain, but I still didn't know what these people wanted from me. What if the reason I couldn't remember was connected back to this place?

"Was I attacked by a shifter?" I pressed again, shifting the subject away.

Instead of answering, Lily stood, taking my arm and urging us toward the exit. "Evie, I'm going to show her to her house so she can wash up a bit before tonight. I'll see you tomorrow for the shift?"

Evie nodded and waved us away, returning to her meal that had gone cold while we were talking.

Lily walked me past a few rows of cottages until we came to one almost directly in front of the Alpha's log mansion. Something told me that wasn't an accident.

Stepping in through the unlocked door, I took stock of the place. It was more modern than I expected, given what the outside looked like. A modest living room greeted us, fully furnished with a black leather couch and television. There were no plugs I could see, and I wondered why they'd put a TV in the room that couldn't be used.

We moved through a modest kitchen equipped with a stainless steel fridge, an electric stove top, and a red wooden dining table propped in one corner. A small clock blinked the time at me in rigid blue numbers.

"How does this place get electricity?" I questioned Lily.

"Witches." She winked at my expression, sauntering out of the kitchen and back through the living room. At the thought, another burning question popped into my head.

"Do witches heal people? Is that why I didn't die in the attack?"

Lily glanced back at me, her face unreadable. "I know you have more questions, but please let Wolfe answer that one. He will kill me once he finds out how much I already told you. You have no reason to trust me," she continued, leading the way through the house. "But I promise you, he will answer your questions."

I debated badgering her further, but a part of me believed her. She'd shown me so much already; I'd admit I liked her if I wasn't lying to myself.

I resigned myself to let it go as we turned into the only other room in the house, the bedroom.

It was larger than I expected, boasting a massive king-size bed in the center. There were no linens, but two clear plastic bags sat on the edge, which I'd bet money on had blankets and pillows inside. A small ensuite bathroom was off to the left with a clinically clean shower and tub combo inside.

"Every pack member gets a house, or a family house depending on their needs. As I said, Wolfe keeps us safe. While you're here with us, you're safe."

"Safe from what?" I asked.

"The world is a dangerous place." I didn't mistake the graveness in her voice, only capable of coming from someone who had experienced painful losses in their life. "It's safer for us to stick together."

She gestured to the clock on the nightstand. Half past twelve. "I'll come back and get you at six for dinner. Feel free to get washed up. We put your backpack in the closet." With a last pointed look at my outfit that had seen better days, she left the cottage, and for the first time all day, I was alone.

I sank to the edge of the bed, my mind a whirlwind trying to process everything I had learned. The shifters were real, and they wanted me to stay with them. I was too old to be a shifter and felt absolutely human, so why would they keep me here?

Lily hadn't confirmed it, but I was reasonably convinced my attacker hadn't been human. My memory was hazy, but that wolf had been much larger than any wolf should be, larger than Lily, who was already pushing the scale as it was.

Maybe they wanted to keep me quiet? But that didn't really make sense, given Lily and Evie had just spent the last hour telling me their secret. No, it had to be something else. And I still needed to know why I wasn't dead on the side of the road right now.

I resolved to ask Wolfe as many questions as humanly possible.

I'd get my answers and that car, and then I was gone.

Chapter Five

I took a long bath, sinking into the heated water as my tense muscles unknotted one by one. My newfound stress was starting to take its toll, and it had been less than twenty-four hours. After toweling off, I laid down on the bed, intending to nap for only a few hours and regain my strength. I had a long night of driving ahead of me once I left tonight.

I woke suddenly, startled to see it was beginning to get dark outside. Glancing at the clock, I realized I had about ten minutes before Lily was due to show up. I rushed to the closet, relieved to see my backpack lying on the floor. I rummaged through the bag, pulling out a fresh pair of underwear and a plain gray T-shirt. After more rummaging, I let out a curse. In my haste, I'd completely forgotten to pack a change of pants. I looked down at my stained, ripped jeans I'd thrown into a heap on the floor and sighed. Dirty pants it is.

I was running my fingers through my blonde locks like a makeshift brush, trying to remove the knots that had settled in during my nap, when a cheerful knock sounded at the door.

Lily gave my jeans a reproachful look but said nothing, and we set off directly behind the house and towards the mansion at its back. The large oval door was opened by none other than Wolfe himself, wearing a similarly casual outfit to mine, minus the car accident residue. The man, the myth, the Alpha.

He smiled down at me warmly, decidedly not looking at my pants. "Rowan! I'm glad to see you didn't run away yet. Thank you, Lily. I'll take it from here." I stepped in without a word, and she closed the door firmly behind me, cementing my fate. I assumed Lily had reported back almost immediately on what had transpired.

I looked around the large foyer I found myself in before following Wolfe through various rooms as he led me to what I hoped was the dining area. I was starving. The mansion had impressively high ceilings, made of the same wooden logs as the outside. From the front, it had looked like multiple floors from the outside, but now I realized it was only one. The house was decorated in a way that told me Wolfe was probably single.

We finally arrived at the dining room, a long grey wooden table with benches along the sides, the only furniture in the room. A large spread was already laid out on top. Two places were already made at one corner of the table, and my mouth watered as I took in the delicious feast.

"Please, have a seat. I can't let a beautiful woman starve, now can I?" I looked at him but said nothing, caught off guard by his flirty nature. I figured the leader of a pack of shifters would be more serious.

He escorted me to one of the two empty chairs and pulled it out for me to sit before taking his own—the perfect gentleman.

I devoured the spread with my eyes. The table was decorated with succulent ribeye, brussels sprouts, and a large bowl of mashed potatoes; way more than two people should need. I bet it took a lot of food to keep a shifter happy, and I glanced at him, wondering what animal he turned into. I had to assume wolf for obvious reasons.

Wolfe watched me with an amused look, like a child who had been let loose in a candy store.

"Eat," he urged me, pushing the plate adorned with ribeye closer to me.

I tried to hold out and not seem desperate, but the food was screaming at me to eat it.

I piled my plate high, stuffing my face immediately. I am sure I looked unhinged, but the last thing on my mind right now was trying to catch a new man. After Chad, I might even swear off boys forever. A pang of hurt slid through me at the reminder.

Keep your eye on the prize Rowan.

"Who attacked me?" I asked bluntly, shifting gears. I wasn't here to make small talk. Wolfe stiffened, not expecting me to go for the jugular with my first question. I narrowed my eyes at him, ready to storm out if he didn't answer. He regarded me cautiously before answering.

"We believe it was a wolf shifter," he said finally. "When Lily told me how you reacted to her change...well, that just seems the most likely culprit."

"You mean you didn't know before?"

"We had our ideas, but I have very few wolves in this pack," Wolfe replied, confirming my suspicions that they hadn't seen my attacker. "Lily is one of only a handful of others, and I know none who are capable of these atrocities."

"There have been other attacks?" I asked.

"Two. Well, three, including yours." He looked sad as he said it, the first time I had really seen his cheery façade falter. Something more was going on here.

"They died?"

"Yes. Except for you." The flirty demeanor was gone now as he pinned me with his stare. We locked eyes, and I held his gaze for longer than was probably necessary, but intuition told me I needed to. My brow furrowed, and I felt sweat bead on my forehead. After what felt like forever, I broke eye contact, my breath whooshing out of my body. I had lost a contest I didn't even understand I was playing. I didn't miss the shock that flitted across Wolfe's face.

"Why am I here?" I asked again, hoping this time I'd get an answer.

"We need your help," he looked at me with a serious expression. "This rogue wolf is terrorizing us and the nearby packs, and you're the only person to have survived an attack and lived to tell the tale. You saw it."

"Cool, I'll draw you a picture and be on my way." I looked around as if for a pen and paper to do exactly that, but his bark of laughter made me focus back on him.

"Why am I still alive?" I questioned, shifting my body forward to lean on the table.

"This is where you belong, Rowan." His happy mask was back on again, and I was tempted to punch the smile off his face. I didn't have anywhere I belonged; that was my thing.

"I'm not a shifter, I'm too old. Did you heal me?"

He leaned forward, his grey eyes calculating. "I'll tell you how you were healed if you tell me how you protected yourself."

I glared at him. "What? Didn't one of your people chase off the wolf?"

"You still can't remember what happened?" He shook his head. "By the time we got to you, you were by yourself. You had to have protected yourself."

"I don't really remember most of it," I blurted out honestly, hoping I wasn't telling him too much. "I assumed one of your people protected me."

"Callan, the shifter who found you, said there was no one else. You must have fought them off."

I threw my head back and laughed. "I did not do any fighting. Not against that thing." He squinted at me like I was a riddle he was trying to solve but couldn't. Finally, he sighed, running his hands through his unruly mop of hair with his signature move.

"You were already healing on your own when you got to us. The smell of shifter is all over you." His nostrils flared as he spoke, and I flushed red. Of course, shifters would have an acute sense of smell.

"I'm twenty-three," I protested. I didn't want to get hopeful and think there could be anything special about me.

"I think I can help trigger your shift tomorrow night during the full moon."

"You've got the wrong person."

"I've got the right person," he said firmly, and I felt a small burst of butterflies erupt in my belly at his words. He continued, "Let me help you, and then you can help us. A favor."

"Favor is just a fancy word for debt."

I didn't want to sound ungrateful. I was very glad I still had my life, but I didn't belong here. Even if I did turn into some mysterious animal, this wasn't my home. I didn't have a house or a family to go back to. I'd always been a lone wolf, no pun intended, and I planned to keep it that way.

He regarded me thoughtfully, and I flushed under the heat of his gaze as he looked me up and down. I may not be into this whole shifter thing, but I was still a hot-blooded woman and knew when a guy was checking me out. Chad was barely a blip on the radar at this point.

"What if I sweeten the pot?" he asked in a conspiratorial whisper like we were old friends planning a prank and not talking about tracking down a werewolf serial killer. He leaned in closer to me, his face only inches away.

"I told you I'm not interested. Now, where is that car you promised me?" I scooted my chair back, more to create distance than anything else. Being that close to my face, I could smell him, like a mix of warm amber and vanilla.

"Ten thousand dollars."

"What?"

There was an unmistakable sparkle in his eye. "If you can help lead us to the killer, I'll give you ten thousand dollars and the car. In the meantime, you can stay here for free."

My eyes narrowed at him. He knew my weaknesses and was catering to them like a Michelin-star chef. My first instinct was to say no, but the more I thought about it, the more I realized I couldn't. I acted tough, but the reality was that I had nothing: no car, no money, and no purpose. Ten thousand dollars would be enough to get me started somewhere completely new.

And what if what he said was true? Was I really a shifter? If it proved true, maybe I could figure out what I was and where I'd come from. I needed answers. What did I have to lose?

Chapter Six

Wolfe was ecstatic to hear I accepted the offer. He walked me home after dinner, leaving me on my doorstep with a friendly goodnight. We made plans to meet up again the next day, a few hours before the pack was set to shift.

I tossed and turned all night, dreams riddled with snarling attacking wolves. In every dream, I felt a cold, seeping darkness sweep over me, snuffing out the wolves from my mind's eye. By the time the sun rose, the golden haze filtering through the blinds, I was staring at the ceiling, contemplating all the bad choices I had made that had led me here.

A knock on my door startled me, but I quickly jumped into some clothes and opened the door.

"Good morning!" A very chipper Lily stood at the door, a drink carrier in one hand and a brown paper bag in the other. I glowered at her, attempting to shut the door in her face. I was not a morning person, even on my most well-rested days. Lightning quick, she darted a foot out and blocked the door.

"Nice try, but you'll have to do better than that if you want to keep me out. Shifter reflexes." She waggled her eyebrows at me, and I couldn't help the smile that escaped me. Something about Lily made me feel at ease, melting my tough exterior just a bit.

Lily smiled at my amusement, and I quickly schooled my expression back into grumpus mode. I couldn't let her think I was actually a nice person. The delicious aroma of cinnamon and bread wafted out of the bag she held. My nose scented the air like a dog.

"Please tell me that's a cinnamon raisin bagel."

A bemused look crossed her face. "You're sense of smell is getting stronger."

I shook my head before I snatched the bag out of her hand. "I just really like bagels."

She snorted before entering the house and shutting the door softly behind her. After opening the bag and confirming there was indeed a delicious bagel, I snatched one cup of coffee she held and downed it immediately before taking the second one from her as well. If there was one thing you got from working at a coffee shop, it was an outrageous tolerance for caffeine at unsafe temperatures.

Lily said nothing even though I had stolen her coffee for myself. Her dark eyes regarded me curiously, and I noticed her nostrils flair slightly as she watched me.

"What do I smell like?" I implored, hoping she didn't say something gross like BO. It seemed like random people sniffing me would be something I had to get used to here. I couldn't wait to solve this mystery and be gone.

"It's hard to pinpoint. You smell of shifter; that much is obvious. But there's something else. Something...I don't know. Different," she said, although she didn't seem satisfied with the word she chose. "I've never met someone who smelled like you before."

I quirked an eyebrow. "I think you just haven't smelled a human in a while."

"Are you always this way?"

"Beautiful, charming, enchanting?" I batted my eyelashes at her.

"Difficult," she said finally, but with a small smile, so I knew she was joking.

I looked off into the distance, pretending to ponder before turning back to her with a grin. "Yes."

She might have been able to see the back of her head with how hard she rolled her eyes.

"Come on; you're going to help me set up for tonight."

"So what is this thing anyway?" I asked as Lily and I sat down in the cafeteria to eat lunch, again joining Evie all by her lonesome at her usual corner table. We'd spent the better part of the morning cleaning, mowing, and organizing the entire compound, and all I could glean was that everyone was freaking out about it. Dozens of people milled about as they each worked on their various tasks to prepare for the night.

"It's a festival of sorts," Evie answered, greeting me with a wide smile.

"We hold one of these every month on the full moon. We can shift whenever we want, but the urge is incredibly hard to fight on the full moon. So we gather all together, and we shift as a family." There it was again, that word family. They used it so often that this almost sounded like a cult. Next, they'd tell me Wolfe had six wives, one for each day of the week, and I was to be the seventh.

"Each pack takes turns hosting it. We neighbor three other packs nearby, Avenwood, Allentown, and Seaville. This month is our turn."

"Are the other packs part of the family, too?"

Lily threw back her head and laughed, a melodious sound. Evie just smirked to herself. "No. Each separate pack is its own unit. And not all packs are as nice as this one. Each pack is run by an Alpha, the most dominant shifter. Unfortunately, sometimes dominance comes along with arrogance. Wolfe is one of the good ones."

"Then why do the other packs come?"

"For mating." This time it was Evie who answered, a dreamy expression crossing her face.

"Mating?" I asked incredulously. "Oh my god, is this a giant orgy?"

Anxiety spiked in me at the thought. I had some experience, but I was by no means an expert. Chad and a sloppy high school boyfriend were the only two entries on my list of men who had been to my land down under, and no one was winning any awards.

"Finding mates," Evie clarified, her cheeks beet red against her pale skin. "We invite the other packs over because we may find our mates."

Seeing my confusion, Lily continued, "Shifters' mates are found when we are in our animal form. It's like a draw, an instant connection. The fates tie you together."

"And you're stuck with this person for the rest of your life? You don't even know them, but you're expected to love them?" Being forced to be with someone just because an invisible force said so sounded hellish. I don't think I could ever love someone at first sight.

Lily looked offended at my questions. "It's a sacred tradition, driven by the same magic that gives us the abilities to do what we can. It's fate's will."

"At my first shift last month, I saw three different mates find each other," Evie said wistfully. "It's really beautiful, and I can't wait for that day to come for me."

I stared at them both, wondering how they had become so delusional.

"I don't get it, I'm sorry."

Lily patted my hand, a pitying look in her eye. "It's okay, you will soon. You have a mate out there somewhere, too."

I was saved from having to respond when a gruff voice interrupted us.

"Lily, Wolfe is asking for you." A tall, dark, and handsome

type stood at our table, his hazel eyes bearing down at us. He had a similar air of power that Wolfe did but not as strong, wafting around him in mild waves. Evie blushed and looked down at her plate, pushing the food around listlessly with her fork.

"Malachi!" Lily rejoiced, her face lighting up when she looked at him. It wasn't romantic, more like a couple of old friends catching up. "Have you met our newest recruit?"

"Temporary recruit," I corrected her. I had a job to do, and then I was leaving, ten thousand dollars richer. I almost drooled at the thought.

Malachi turned to me, and we locked eyes, and again I was locked into a staring contest I didn't sign up for. His brow furrowed as the seconds stretched on before he finally broke the contact and looked away, a low growl escaping his throat.

"Wolfe, now!" he barked before turning on his heel and leaving.

We all sat in silence, both girls looking at me with surprise.

"What?" I was sick of everyone looking at me, like I was a lab experiment they were about to dissect.

"I have to go," Lily said, getting up from her seat in a hurry, trying not to meet my eyes. "Wolfe is waiting. Meet me back here at six; wear something comfortable."

She was gone before I even had a chance to react. I was getting really frustrated that they only told me things when they wanted me to know. Huffing a breath, I turned my attention to Evie, eyes narrowed.

"What happened just now?" Evie balked, going sheet white and avoiding my eyes.

"Evie," I emphasized, my stare boring a hole in her head, willing her to tell me what was going on. "Please. No one tells me anything and I need to know. Don't you remember how it was when you were new?"

She looked me over, and I saw the resolve change in her eyes as she took pity on me. She sighed. "Fine, but you didn't get this information from me. Wolfe told us not to tell you too much yet.

He doesn't want us to scare you away." Her eyes widened as she realized she probably shouldn't have let that slip. I took a deep breath, compartmentalizing my anger for later when I saw Wolfe.

"It's okay," I lied. "Just tell me."

"The staring contests that you keep getting into? That's how we shifters determine dominance. Alpha power. The longer you can hold a stare, the more dominant you are. I know my place in the pack is towards the bottom because I can't hold a gaze for very long. Lily too. We're what they call submissives."

"Okay..." I said, waiting for her to get to the point.

"Malachi is the beta, Wolfe's second in command. You haven't even shifted yet, and you just beat him in a dominance contest."

Chapter Seven

Evie and I parted ways after that little revelation, me retiring back to my little house to get ready for the night. I didn't want to think that I had out-dominated the second in command because that would mean I'd have to think that maybe I was going to shift into an animal tonight. I didn't want to think about any of this, really. The more I learned about these people, the more it seemed like I was one of them, and I didn't want that to be true. I wanted to drive off into the sunset, live in a beach house, and enjoy my simple life of solitude all by my lonesome. I was in over my head, and I knew it.

Six o'clock came too fast, and I took my precious time throwing on another T-shirt from my bag. A pair of jeans had been dropped on my bed with the tags still on them when I'd returned from the cafeteria, and I was grateful I didn't have to wear my disgusting ones again. Once I had my ten thousand, the first thing I was going to do was some retail therapy. I missed my usual uniform of combat boots and a black leather jacket.

By the time I moseyed my way back to the mess hall, the festivities were in full swing. There was double the number of people I usually saw and faces I didn't recognize; the sound of children running and playing slightly warmed my cold dead heart.

I had thought all packs didn't have many children, but I now realized that was an assumption I had made. Why did this pack have fewer children than the others?

Lily stood by the entrance, an especially irate expression marring her flawless face.

"You're late," she said flatly, meeting my eyes for a second before quickly averting. Now that it had been pointed out to me, I became more aware of all the people I had inadvertently stared down over the past few days. The only one to have made me look away was Wolfe—that secret-keeping bastard.

"Does that mean I don't have to go anymore?" I retorted. I didn't have any apologies left in me; I survived solely off caffeine and attitude. She was lucky I even showed up.

Her expression softened. "I'm sorry I didn't tell you." Wow, Evie could not keep a secret.

"When the Alpha tells you to do something, you do it. There's no room for questioning it."

"If he told you to jump off a cliff, would you do that too?" I sounded like a middle-aged parent, but it was a valid question.

"Absolutely," she said loyally. I just shook my head; this was definitely a cult. I see now why she was a submissive wolf.

"I have to tell you something. We have a surprise guest tonight." She told me in hushed tones, changing the subject. She steered me off toward one of the recreational buildings, a small one off to one corner. "The Supreme Alpha is here. That's why I had to leave earlier. Wolfe needed my help to get some things for him."

"The Supreme Alpha? Why should I care?"

"He's the Alpha of all Alphas here in the US. You should very much care, as he's here to see you." She rolled her eyes as if I had said the most outrageous thing she'd ever heard.

"Me? Why the heck would he want to see me?"

"Well, not just you. Wolfe wants you both in there."

"Both?"

"You and Callan. And you were supposed to be there 20

minutes ago," she said grimly. She stopped walking, and I realized we had reached the entrance to the meeting room. "I'm not allowed to go in there with you. I know you don't trust us yet, but please, whatever you do, do not get into a staring contest in there. It's for your own good," she said before pushing me through the door, shutting it firmly behind me.

Three pairs of eyes turned to land on me when the door sounded, and I gulped, entirely unprepared for the assault of power thickening the air of the small room. Wolfe stood in the center, and I could feel his power assault my senses with the force of his anger. I wasn't sure if it was at me for being late or because of the gigantic man that stood before him.

If I thought Wolfe was large with his seven-foot clearance and broad, hulking shoulders, this man was a fucking castle. He towered over Wolfe by at least six inches, his arm muscles bulging so large they might need their own zip code. He was middle-aged with a close-cropped buzz cut, and I realized most of the power I felt in the room emanated from him. It was almost suffocating, my lungs struggling to push past the sheer oppressiveness of it as it filled the tiny room. I'd bet my left tit that this was the Supreme Alpha.

Another man stood a small way behind Wolfe. He was half a foot shorter than Wolfe and almost the exact opposite regarding physicality. Where Wolfe was broad and hulking, filling up any room he walked into, this man was long and lean, his tight muscles flexing subtly under his black thermal sweater. He projected calm, but his body language told me he was not one to mess with, coiled and ready to strike at a moment's notice.

Under a mop of jet-black hair, emerald-green eyes met mine, and I gasped as the force of his own power collided with me, swirling and wrapping around me. The midnight caress was a grateful respite from the fiery heat of the other two Alphas in the room. If I didn't know any better, I would have said it was examining me. This must be Callan, the rogue shifter. Remembering what Lily said about eye contact, I quickly averted my gaze, and the power dissipated almost immediately.

"Rowan, come!" Wolfe ordered, gesturing for me to join him in the center of the room. Gone was the cheerful, flirtatious man I had eaten dinner with. There was only the Alpha left standing in his place. "You're late enough as it is."

I narrowed my eyes at the command. Besides the bone I had to pick with him, I didn't appreciate being bossed around. If he thought I would fall in line like Lily, he had another thing coming to him.

"It's hard to be on time for something that no one tells you about," I told him pointedly, crossing my arms and making no move to get any closer. "And don't give me orders. If you want me to do something, you can say please or nothing at all."

The silence in the room was deafening, and I tensed, unsure if I had gotten myself into more trouble than it was worth. I had no doubt it would only take one of these guys to punch my lights out. A burst of laughter broke out, deep and hearty, from the Supreme Alpha. He slapped a meaty hand on Wolfe's shoulder, harder than was friendly.

"This is how you let your shifters speak to you, Alpha Gregory? Maybe we should be discussing your future as an Alpha as well."

"I'm not one of his," I spat. "I'm not a shifter at all."

The Supreme laughed again, and I sensed the dark undertone in his voice. This man was not amused at all. He tried to lock his gray eyes with mine, and, remembering my warning, I focused on the spot right between his eyes. He smiled sinisterly, lumbering over to stand directly in front of me. I forced myself not to back down. I would heed the warning about eye contact, but I would not let this man intimidate me into submission.

The Supreme reached a hand up to touch a lock of my hair, and I cringed away, a low growl sounding behind him from Wolfe as he grabbed a strand. "Yes, you are, little one. You smell. . . so good," he said, leaning down to sniff the lock of my hair he held. I fought the urge to run as far away as I could. "How unique."

"Don't touch her, Duke," Wolfe growled, taking a menacing step forward. The Supreme Duke dropped my hair, instantly forgotten as he pivoted to face Wolfe.

"You will refer to me as Supreme Alpha Gregory," he commanded, his power suffocating Wolfe's as they battled for dominance. My eyes widened as I connected the dots. This was Wolfe's father. He had to be. Looking at them both now, I realized Wolfe was just a younger, more handsome version of the Supreme. Talk about family problems.

"Enough." The low voice came from Callan, who had been watching the entire exchange blankly. As he spoke, I could hear the tinge of a Scottish accent, which I might have been swooning over if I wasn't busy questioning my existence. "Why did you call us here?"

The Supreme relaxed his tension slowly, not taking his eyes off Wolfe until the very last moment.

"These killings need to stop," he said finally. "The Alpha Council is getting very concerned that you are in way over your head, Alpha Gregory. Two dead shifters in your region in the last two months. I'm here to fix your mess."

Wolfe looked outraged. "How is this my fault? Those shifters weren't even in my pack. I'm doing all I can to help the other Alphas figure out who is doing this."

The Supreme looked at him with disgust. "Not your fault? You are my son, no matter how much you want to deny it. How will you become the Supreme Alpha when I'm gone if you can't even deal with a rogue shifter when he's right under your nose?"

"Callan isn't responsible for this," Wolfe said firmly, shifting to angle his body between Callan and the Supreme in a protective stance. Callan's indifferent expression intrigued me, given he was being accused of being a serial killer right to his face. It didn't seem like he even cared.

"You are the only Alpha with a rogue shifter living on their outskirts, especially one with his history. Two dead and no witnesses. I allowed Callan to stay as a favor to you, but you've abused my graciousness. Your blind trust is costing people their lives."

"It wasn't him!" Wolfe shouted at his father. Still, Callan said nothing to defend himself, his eyes devoid of emotion. "Someone else is responsible for this."

"It wasn't Callan," I confirmed, and all eyes shot to me, including Callan's. I cleared my throat under the sudden attention before continuing. "I was attacked two days ago by a wolf shifter."

I caught Callan's eye briefly, his eyes darkening until they almost looked black. I looked away hastily, feeling awkward under his scrutiny.

"There was another attack?" the Supreme questioned, expression thundering.

"Why didn't you tell me?" he roared, again turning on Wolfe. Wolfe bristled, patches of dark brown fur erupting on his arms and neck before he took a deep, steadying breath, the fur slowly dissolving back into his skin. Had he almost shifted?

I decided to trudge on before we had a full-on shifter showdown in a tiny room that would get me killed in the crossfire. "Yes. I was driving and was run off the road when something cut me off, and I swerved. My attacker was a wolf. Something must have scared it off because the next thing I knew, I was waking up here."

"You're sure it was a wolf?" This came from Callan. My heart skipped a beat as I met his eyes, but I continued, breaking eye contact before I forced a challenge. His question confirmed my suspicions; he had not seen what attacked me before he arrived. So, what had stopped it from killing me?

"Yes," I said. "It looked like Lily, but bigger and reddish brown."

"Why are you still alive?" the Supreme asked bluntly. "If Callan didn't see the attacker, it must have been scared off by something, or else you'd be dead."

I looked down at my shoes, pondering that for a moment. "I don't know. It bit me twice, and I was on the verge of passing out. I think I did. I can't remember anything after that."

"It bit you?" the Supreme Alpha questioned, his intense stare making me squirm.

"Of course, it bit me," I stated, failing to resist the urge to roll my eyes at the stupid question. "It was a wolf."

"None of the other victims were bitten," he said gravely, his eyes flicking between me and Callan. "Why did it attack you differently?"

The question was on the tip of my tongue, almost too afraid to ask, but I needed to know.

"How did they die?" I finally questioned.

"Their hearts were torn from their chests."

My mind raced from that revelation, more confused than ever. If the other victims hadn't been bitten, then why had I? How did we even know it was the same attacker? For all we know, two rogue shifters could be running around out there, attacking people. A sliver of doubt sliced through me, and I shifted my eyes to Callan.

"How did you know the murders were committed by a shifter at all, then? If they weren't bitten, I mean. Or that this was even the same person." The look they all gave me told me that was a stupid question.

"No human has the strength to do what this animal did, Rowan," Wolfe told me, his eyes softening as he looked at me. "Count yourself lucky you weren't one of the bodies. Hopefully, you can give us some clues after your first shift."

"She's never shifted?" Callan questioned; his interest piqued again.

"Not yet," Wolfe confirmed. "That's the other thing. Her shifter gene seemed not to have surfaced until her attack. She's twenty-three."

The looks of shock on their faces would have been comical if I wasn't the cause. I resisted the urge to melt into a puddle on the floor under all their scrutiny.

"But her scent . . ." the Supreme started before trailing off, seemingly lost in thought.

"I'm right here," I said indignantly. I was tired of them talking about me like I couldn't hear every word.

"She's the only one who has scented the attacker directly. That's why I brought her here, so she can help us solve this. I'm hoping we can retroactively identify the attacker once she shifts." Wolfe sounded almost pleading, his attention fully focused on his father.

"I'm still not convinced it isn't this ... rogue. You know what he's capable of." I saw Callan almost imperceptibly stiffen from the corner of my eye, his eyes trained on the Supreme, heat burning in his emerald gaze. That seemed to have struck a chord. "Maybe he enlisted a witch, disguising his form."

"Callan is innocent, and I would bet my life on that." Wolfe stood tall, his words laced with his power as he spoke his conviction.

The Supreme cocked his head, a small smirk playing across his lips as he leveled his son with a menacing look. "You wouldn't be the first person to entrust their life to him and lose."

A growl ripped through the room, and I felt my heart thud in my chest as a sliver of fear coursed through me. This was different from what I had heard from Wolfe earlier. This was the growl of a predator, and I watched Callan carefully, not daring to move.

He was still human, but inky black fur had erupted over his arms, his mouth and chin elongating into what I could almost call a muzzle. His eyes were brighter than ever, orbs of glowing green flecked with gold that hadn't been there before. He didn't move. He didn't need to. We all knew he was one second away from ripping someone's throat out, judging by the claws that had taken over his fingers. I didn't know exactly what he was, but it was far from a wolf, of that I was certain.

No one spoke; the Supreme and Callan locked in a death

stare. The silence stretched on for what seemed like an eternity, sweat beading on both of their brows as they fought for control, the flames of the Supreme's power battling against Callan's icy intensity, neither showing signs of giving in. It seemed like all these men liked to do was get angry and stare each other down. I waited a few more seconds for them to put their dicks away, but it didn't happen.

"OKAY!" I shouted, clapping my hands together as loud as I possibly could. Surprisingly the distraction worked as all three men turned to look at me, Callan's fearsome animal form blending back into the human I had first met. "This has been fun. Really, so much fun. We should do this again sometime."

I turned my back on them, intending to walk out the door and never look back. A lightly accented voice stopped me in my tracks.

"*Rowan.*" It was barely above a whisper, but I heard it. A shiver traced down my spine as I turned back around. I looked at Callan, but he just stared his blank look back at me, and I began to doubt if he had even said my name in the first place.

Wolfe looked between me and Callan for a moment, a frown furrowing his brow before he turned back to his father. He opened his mouth to speak, but his father cut him off first.

"I'll give you two more months. If you don't hand the culprit over to me by that time, I will be back here in full force. And trust me, Alpha Gregory, if I have to come back here again and do your job, you will no longer be an Alpha. You will be replaced, and you both will return to Montana with me where you belong."

The Supreme stepped around me on his way out the door. Right before he exited, he turned back, focusing on me, and I noticed his nose flare as he inhaled my scent.

"And she'll come with us." He winked at me before walking out, the door slamming firmly shut behind him as he sealed my fate.

Chapter Eight

"I don't want her help." Callan was the first one to speak, his tone flat. Wolfe's shoulders slumped, exhaustion seeping from his pores. It seemed this wasn't the first time they'd had this argument.

"You don't have a choice, Cal. You've been getting nowhere alone, and you know it."

My ears perked. "You've been investigating on your own already?"

Callan cut his eyes over to me, disdain written on his face. "Yes, and I was doing just fine before you came along. I don't need deadweight slowing me down."

He was lucky I had seen the scary half-shift he did because the urge to punch him in the face was strong. The only thing holding me back was the certainty of the death I knew he could bring.

I pinned him with a glare, forgetting that I shouldn't be picking a fight for dominance. "If you were doing so well on your own, there wouldn't be two people dead."

It took him only seconds to cross the room, coming to a halt directly before me. He was so tall I had to crane my neck upwards to look at him. I'd picked this fight, and now I had to see it through, no matter how much I regretted it.

"Do not challenge me." His gaze burned into mine, and I tried not to notice the flecks of gold swirling in his irises.

I said nothing, focusing all my effort on holding his gaze. The pressure to look away steadily increased, and I knew I couldn't hold out much longer.

Seeing something in my eyes, he smirked. He was more dominant than me, and he knew it. I clenched my teeth with effort before I yanked my eyes away, my breath huffing out of me unsteadily. That was the longest I'd ever challenged anyone so far. I hazarded a glance at him and caught a brief second of what I thought was an appraising look before he shut back down.

"Are you done?" Wolfe wore a sour expression on his face, not amused by our staring contest. "If you won't do it for yourself, then do it for me."

"I owe you nothing," Callan sniffed.

"Nothing? Really, Cal? I'm the one who convinced Duke to let you stay here in the first place! If it was up to him, you would be dead right now. I saved your life." My eyes darted back and forth between them, wishing I had a bucket of popcorn to munch on. There was a lot of bad blood and history between these two.

"Its thanks to me that you're even in this position in the first place," Callan replied, narrowing a glare at Wolfe. "You wouldn't even be an Alpha if it wasn't for me."

They both bristled, jaws clenching as they glared at each other.

"I don't know what's going on between you two and frankly, I don't give a rat's ass. What does concern me is one thing. I was promised ten thousand dollars and a car if I help you find this killer. You are not messing that up for me. No one said we had to do this together, so if you don't want to work with me, then get out of my way."

I had no idea how I was supposed to catch an animal-shifting serial killer, but the money was an opportunity I couldn't pass up. I had to at least try.

They both stared at me with their mouths open before Wolfe

laughed loudly. For a split second, Callan's mouth quirked upwards slightly. The rest of the tension eased out of the room in time with Wolfe's subsiding laughter. A companionable silence kicked in for a few moments before someone spoke again.

"She can't do it on her own. You know she's going to get herself killed with that attitude." Wolfe shot Callan a pleading look.

Callan regarded me again before letting out the breath he'd been holding in. "Fine, but if you mess this up, I'll kill you myself."

I couldn't tell if he was joking, but he certainly looked capable of it.

"Come, Rowan," Wolfe said again, no command this time. He slung an arm around my shoulder as we walked out of the meeting room. I dodged under it, not wanting him to touch me when I was still upset with him. "The full moon will be at its strongest soon. Let's see if we can get you to shift. Can you feel it calling to you?"

I didn't, but the question was rhetorical because he turned his head over his shoulder to talk behind him as we exited. "Run with the packs tonight. You won't make it home in time for the pull."

Now outside, Callan turned his face towards the moon but said nothing, the brilliant white orb casting a glow over his features. I found myself studying him, questions racing through my brain as I digested everything I had heard tonight. This man had a dark past, that was for sure. Wolfe seemed confident in his innocence, but I had just met this man today.

The festivities were starting to die down; everyone made their way off the property towards a large clearing in a break in the woods.

"Oh my god," I said as we started to near, my brain burning with the imprint of dozens of people in various states of undress as they all stripped naked.

Wolfe gave me a sly grin, still urging me forward, Callan trailing behind us. "It's uncomfortable the first few times you do it, but you'll get used to it. It's much more cost-effective than having to buy new clothes every time."

"I still don't believe anything is going to happen," I told him. "You're going to realize soon how silly this whole thing is. I'm still not convinced I didn't dream this whole thing up."

"Are you always this difficult?"

I blinked up at him. "You're the second person to ask me that today."

He winked at me, but I ignored it. I was not in a mood to be charmed. "There's Lily. Find a spot. I have to go play good host. I'll be back." He jogged off in the vague direction of the front of the clearing.

I looked around, spotting Lily. Even in a crowd of people, she stuck out. I started over to her before remembering Callan hovering nearby. "You coming?"

He looked out at the people around the circle, hesitation written on his face. I looked around, noticing more than one angry look being shot in his direction.

"I shouldn't have come here tonight," he said, his expression again tightening up into his mask.

"Why aren't you part of the pack?" After hearing what the Supreme had said to him, it had been running through my mind. He looked at me briefly before averting his gaze, scanning the crowd. I was getting nothing out of him.

I stomped towards where I saw Lily in the crowd at the back of the clearing. When she saw me, her face lit up, and I felt a little bad I had been so short with her earlier. She was doing what she thought she was supposed to, no matter how misguided it was. The person I should really be mad at was Wolfe.

I thought I was alone until her expression switched, looking both nervous and strangely intrigued as she saw something behind me.

"Why did Callan come back with you?" She whispered to me as I got up to her before he was within earshot. I shook my head, giving her a pointed look that said we'd discuss it later.

"I'll stay in the back, don't worry," Callan said to Lily, stepping back a few feet so we had plenty of space.

Lily was already naked, and I kept my eyes firmly on her face as we chatted.

"I'm going to help him find who's been killing those shifters," I told her.

She nodded her head. "Wolfe told me the details about your attack, that you saw who did it. I'm glad you made it out okay," she said, reaching over and squeezing my hand. I returned it and dropped her hand, feeling something warm and fuzzy in my chest that I didn't care to identify.

"So, what's supposed to happen now?" I asked her.

"When the moon reaches its peak in a few minutes, you will feel a pull on you to change. It starts low, in your belly. Don't fight it. While you can technically stop the change if you want, it hurts like a bitch. If you do it right, it should only hurt for a few minutes. Just let the magic take you over, and before you know it, you'll be in your true form."

"What if nothing happens?" I was about to ask a million more questions when a booming voice rang out, and it took me a moment to realize it was Wolfe. Looking around, I saw him standing at the front of the clearing, slightly elevated above the crowd, standing on a large stone.

"Ladies and gentlemen, friends and family. The Clover pack is excited to welcome you into our fold for tonight's run. I see some new faces out in the crowd. Here's to hoping we find some beautiful new mate pairings!"

The crowd cheered loudly; the sound almost deafening. Lily cheered along with them, and I saw the hope and determination on her face reflected in many of the others. Glancing behind me at Callan, he met my gaze, a hint of something dark in his eyes that I couldn't fathom. Wolfe hopped off the rock, and I saw him start weaving through the crowd of bodies toward me.

The sounds of bones breaking and reforming sounded all over the clearing. I looked around with my jaw hanging open, in awe of all the simultaneous shifts happening. There were no cries of pain even as I heard the cringeworthy sounds coming from their bodies as they bent and reshaped.

A minute later, I was still standing, now surrounded by animals of all types. There were wolves, bears, cats of both the home and jungle variety, coyotes, birds, and monkeys. The list could go on forever. Lily's wolf looked up from the ground next to me, her big brown eyes broadcasting confusion as to why I was still standing.

I searched inside myself, seeing if I had missed a secret hidden animal inside of me somewhere, but nothing seemed out of the ordinary. I tried to ignore the small surge of disappointment that I felt.

"I thought this might happen," Callan said in a low voice behind me. I gasped, rotating around to look at him. I had fully expected him to have shifted with everyone else too. Why was he still standing?

My mind blanked as I saw that while he hadn't shifted, he was certainly ready to, standing completely naked in front of me. My eyes darted down of their own accord, and I flushed red, my eyes snapping back up to his face, trying to get the mental image out of my mind and failing miserably.

He seemed completely unaware, instead approaching me with a purposeful stride. "You're blocked by magic. I can smell it."

Wolfe appeared at my elbow, also having disrobed at some point, and I averted my eyes to the sky. The sound of feet thundered around me before fading as the shifters ran off into the woods to start the night.

"Couldn't you guys have undressed after we did this?" I said, my voice wavering slightly. Wolfe grinned but ignored my comment as he set his hands on my still fully-clothed shoulders.

"Callan is right. Under the full moon, I can smell your animal, but she's trapped. If you allow me, I think I can use my Alpha powers to lift it."

He stood expectantly, waiting for my blessing even as I saw the strain of resisting. I took a deep breath before nodding once.

He wasted no time, gripping my head between his hands and closing his eyes, and I followed suit. My body heated as his fiery power poured into me, coursing through my body. It was comforting until the magic found the locked box in my core. The flames surrounded it, trying to burn away its walls with no response except a searing pain as it burned me instead.

"It won't let me through," Wolfe gritted out. The flames surged hotter, and I cried out in pain.

Another pair of hands gripped the back of my head, and I hissed through my teeth at the cold wash of power that flooded into me. It joined the flames inside, not fighting the other but instead writhing until it formed a solid force ready to strike again. They pushed together, and their combined magic smashed through the barrier without hesitation. I screamed out in pain as I shattered into a million little pieces. I vaguely heard the sound of an animal roar as I broke, but my mind was too fractured to care.

The pain tore through me as if every molecule of my being was being destroyed and reconstructed simultaneously. What felt like hours dragged by before I felt like I was fully whole again.

I opened my eyes, shock coursing through me as I took in the world around me. I looked up, a gigantic wolf towering above me. How did a wolf get this big? The wolf turned its eyes down at me, and I realized with a start that it was Lily. Her tongue lolled out, and she panted. I could have sworn she was laughing at me.

Had I just-? I looked down at my body, my shock coming out in tiny squeaks, not at all like the curses I was trying to sling as I rotated my body side to side, getting a good look at myself. I was a rabbit. A stark white, bushy-tailed rabbit.

A motherfucking rabbit?

A growl erupted from my throat as I tried to air my frustrations, pleased to say I impressed myself with the ferocity of the noise. Lily's wolf bent down and brushed her snout across the top of my head, right between my long, pointed ears.

Use your mind. Her voice echoed in my head. *We can talk to each other in animal form when we touch.*

I placed my small paw on her much larger one and did my best to project my thoughts. *I'm a fucking bunny, Lily. I didn't even get a cool animal like a tiger or a dragon or something.*

Her wolf absolutely grinned at me this time. *Dragons aren't real. Being a bunny can have a lot of advantages—hard to catch, fast, great reflexes. We'll experiment with what you can do later. For now, enjoy the run.*

She tore off into the brush of the surrounding trees, and I just sat there, hesitant to move in my new body. I was still reeling with the fact that I really was a shifter. Remembering, I looked around for Callan and Wolfe.

As I rotated around, I came face to face with a gigantic beast. A black panther sat behind me; golden eyes trained on me. He was entirely black, save for one solid streak of white that went from the top of his head to the tip of his nose. A low rumble sounded from its throat.

I squeaked in fear, backing up, and I almost jumped out of my skin when its heavy paw shot out to pin me to the ground. My fear quickly turned as I angrily squeaked at him.

Shut up, Thumper. Callan's voice floated through my mind, amusement lacing his tone and pissing me off even more.

Let me go, you asshole! I couldn't get a cooler animal than a rabbit?

His amusement was apparent in his voice. *The rabbit was always going to be your animal.*

I narrowed my eyes. I may not be strong, but I was resourceful. Opening wide, I twisted my small body to the side to get a good angle. With all the force I could muster, I bit down on the paw that held me, satisfaction coursing through me as I penetrated the skin.

He let out a roar, and I took advantage of the distraction to wriggle my way out from under his paw and dart off through the nearest break in the trees. I used my size to my advantage, ducking and diving through the small plants and forest life I encountered. I was pleased to see just how fast I could run, not stopping until I was sure I wasn't being followed.

I stopped by a small pond, pausing to look at my reflection in the moonlight. My eyes looked back at me, but my reflection was indeed that of a rabbit. Long, straight ears stood up from my head, my eyes large and round, centered on my face. My body was small but strong, and my tail was nothing more than a small poof on my rear end. From head to toe, I was completely white.

Leaves crunched behind me, and I stiffened, alert. I slowly rotated around, my eyes searching frantically in the dark. Being this small made me much more aware that I was surrounded by predators.

A bear came lumbering out of the brush, walking on all fours slowly towards me. He was huge, at least eight feet tall, and covered in dark brown fur. The only marking was a small white spiral in the center of his chest.

When it got close enough, it lay on its stomach, stretching its arms out toward me in an almost human gesture. Its grey eyes stared into mine expectantly, and I squinted at the familiarity of it. Hesitantly, I hopped forward and laid my paw on the bear's arm.

WOLFE? I asked incredulously. I'd forgotten about him, more concerned with fleeing Callan than anything else.

The bear winked at me. *For all that spunk, I thought you would be a tiger or something. You know, something fierce and menacing.* He looked my small form up and down pointedly before making a chuffing sound that must have been the bear version of a laugh.

You have the gall to laugh at me? I threw back at him. *You turn into a bear, but your name is Wolfe. Did your parents hate you or something?*

I regretted my words immediately as his laughter dried up.

I'm sorry, that wasn't fair. I'm just still pissed at you for not telling me everything. I gave him the best rabbit glare I could muster.

You have the right to be mad at me. That wasn't fair of me either, but I didn't know if we could trust you. From now on, let's have an open-door policy, okay? I promise I'll tell you the truth, the whole truth, and nothing but the truth. I swear on my word as Alpha.

I squinted at him, wondering if I could take his word for it. I'd been lied to so many times in my life that it was hard to trust people. I thought back to all the foster homes I had been in, all the times they had told me it would be the last one just for me to get shipped off to somewhere else when they got tired of me. I searched his eyes for signs of deception but found none, only the earnest gaze of a man trying to make amends. Finally, I nodded my forgiveness.

Now let's enjoy the run. No one will hurt you here. Run free.

He was right. We ran back out into the forest, joining the others as they nipped and played with each other, the unabashed freedom filling my soul as we continued throughout the night. The more I moved, the more comfortable I felt in my new skin. I didn't have the size or power of a big animal, but I could get in and out of areas that most of them didn't even notice.

Lily found me closer to dawn, and together we ran, the squawk of an eagle soaring overhead. I ran until I could no longer, my legs jellied and weak. As the sun rose over the forest, we all piled together in the clearing, falling asleep in our animal forms.

Chapter Nine

My eyes squinted in the bright sunlight as I woke, a sense of rightness in my soul that I'd never felt before. The colors of the forest around me were more vivid and vibrant. Scents drifted through my nose, more sensitive than I was used to. The musky scent of the people around me, the crispness of the freshly tended grass in the clearing. It was like a whole new world.

People milled about the clearing, searching the ground for their clothes. I flushed as I looked down at myself, now human, realizing I was also naked. The embarrassment increased as I realized I was sandwiched between Evie and Lily, and I quickly wrestled myself free and stood up.

Where the heck had my clothes gone? Covering my lady bits as best I could, I shuffled over to where we had been standing the night before. I was pleasantly surprised to see my clothes still intact and pulled them on quickly. It seems the clothes damage rule only applied to larger animals; not fearsome bunnies like me.

A shadow caught my eye, revealing a figure perched upon a tree stump on the edge of the clearing, staring at me. Callan watched me, his intense gaze burning a trail across my skin. I stared back at him, the new changes to my vision more pronounced. I marveled at how much detail I could see on his face. Every fleck of hair, every imperfection. Not that he had very many. The guy could have been cut right out of a magazine.

I walked over to him, stopping a respectable distance away. Even this far away, I inhaled, breathing in his uniquely heady scent. My god, the guy smelled good. An intoxicating mixture of spicy sandalwood and freshly laid earth.

"Shifter looks good on you," he said, his expression unreadable. I didn't know what to say to that, so I didn't.

"Someone didn't want you to find out you were a shifter. That was a big spell you had blocking you. A parent, perhaps?"

"I don't have parents," I told him quietly. At the quirk of his brow, I panicked. "I mean, everyone has parents. Obviously." Real smooth.

"I was left at a fire station when I was born. Placed into foster care, bounced from place to place until I aged out of the system and was on my own. I don't know who my parents are."

He cocked his head, green gaze piercing through me like he was trying to read my soul.

"Interesting," was all he said.

"That's it, that's all you got?"

"I suggest you speak with a witch. They may be able to offer you some clarity, at least as far as the spell." He started walking off in the direction of the compound.

"Where are you going?" I asked, trailing after him. I had to take two steps for his every one to make sure I didn't fall behind.

"To solve a murder," he said confidently, not even sparing me a glance.

"We need to talk first," I protested. "I need to know what you've found out so far. We need to develop a game plan so I can help."

He whirled around so suddenly I almost ran straight into him, barely managing to stop myself before impact.

"We don't need to do anything." His expression was dark, thunder looming just below the surface.

"I'm letting you tag along to get Wolfe off my back, but make no mistake, I don't need your help." Every word dripped with malice. He turned right back around, resuming his trek to who knows where. "Do not get in my way."

I stood shell-shocked for a moment, watching as he walked further away before the anger boiled up inside of me and took over like a blazing inferno. I was not one of those girls that could be ordered around, bullied into following along while the macho male called all the shots. If he thought that would work on me, then he was sorely mistaken.

I ran to catch up to him, surprising myself with the swiftness with which I moved. I gripped his arm and jerked him to face me. I stepped as close as I dared and craned my neck back to look in his face. I wore my angriest glare, trying to light his face on fire with sheer will. "Whether you like it or not, you do need my help. I'm the only one who has seen this thing, and I'm damn sure I can sniff it out now."

Or at least I hoped I could. I reached up and poked a singular finger into his chest, ignoring the heat I felt radiating from his body under my hand.

"I'm not taking no for an answer. We are going to sit down and discuss what you've found out so far, and then we'll determine our next steps. Don't let your ego get in the way of your freedom."

I set off towards the mess hall, not waiting for an answer. The satisfaction was palpable when I heard the heavy thud of his footfalls behind me.

Chapter Ten

All eyes were on us when we entered the room. Many of the shifters from the run had stayed for breakfast, still mingling and chatting with their peers. It struck me how normal everyone looked; no one would have any idea that all of these people could change form at will.

I spotted Lily and Evie at a table, they must have trickled in while Callan and I were talking. Lily caught my eye, and I gave her a small smile, but I guided him to a small table off to the side where no one sat. Hopefully, she understood that I did not want to be bothered right now. As we moved, people gave Callan sharp glances, whispering amongst themselves as we passed. My curiosity about his history grew.

I slid into my seat, eyes trained on Callan as he joined me. A muscle in his jaw twitched, but he still sat down, so I counted it as a win. I interlocked my hands and placed them on the table. It was time to talk business.

"What have you learned so far?"

He narrowed his eyes at my tone, the twitch going into overdrive. "I've been to all of the crime scenes, but they're practically useless. I haven't been able to catch a scent. They all took place on pack property, in places well trafficked, but somehow no one has been able to see or scent the intruder."

That was not good news. I wasn't actually sure I'd be able to recognize the scent again, given I had only smelled it while in my human form, but I had to try at least. Step one: visit the crime scenes.

"How about the victims? Any similarities?"

"Alexandria Bristol of Allentown, sixteen. Sam Lee of Seaville, seventeen," he rambled off his list grimly, entirely from memory.

"They're all teenagers?" I whispered, my heart hurting for the victims and their families. A loose serial killer was one thing, but I couldn't even begin to fathom having to fear for the safety of your children.

Reality hit me as I questioned whether I could actually do this. I talked a big game, but it was beginning to sink in that we were dealing with an actual murderer here—one physically capable of ripping a heart out of a chest. I considered throwing the towel in, quitting altogether, and forgetting this happened.

The more I thought about it, the more I realized I couldn't. The money was a huge incentive but more than that, I wanted to learn about myself. I had just shifted into another being, thrown into this new world and life I didn't know existed. I'm not sure that I even wanted to leave anymore. This place opened up an entirely new set of questions that could lead me to discover more about my birth parents. Chances are someone knew them since one had to be a shifter, if not both.

I had so much to learn about this world, about my new body and what it was capable of. I couldn't just let that go. I would see this thing all the way through for myself. A thought struck me then.

"Wait, if they are all underage, why was I attacked?" It didn't make sense. I was way older than all of those children, which seemed to be an obvious thing that they had in common. Attacking me was breaking the pattern.

"That's the question of the week." He leaned forward,

pressing his forearms down on the table as he came closer, his scent enveloping my senses. "Why you?"

I gulped hard, my palms sweaty as his voice sent a heated arrow straight to my center. *What was wrong with me?*

"That's all I know. The victims didn't have much else in common besides their ages. All packs have been alerted to watch their young closely."

I sighed. That was nothing. He needed my help.

"Can you take me to the crime scenes?" I asked him. "Starting with mine."

"That's pointless; I've already been there," he said flatly.

I rolled my eyes. "Can you get over yourself? Sometimes a different perspective helps. Just humor me."

He glowered at me, and I imagined him plotting all the ways he could cause my death and not have to deal with me anymore. Too bad for him; I was on a mission.

"Let's go then." He got to his feet, looking resigned to his fate. "It's going to take all day."

I gave a side wave to the girls as we left, ignoring the suggestive wink Lily gave me as we passed. If she thought there was some love connection that would come from this, she needed a psychiatrist. I didn't know anything about this guy.

He led me towards a gravel road I hadn't noticed before, and as we walked on, a tall, wrought iron gate came into view. 'Clover Forest' was displayed, its rusted lettering covered in a flaking gold paint. The entire thing seemed to be in disrepair, badly needing a refresh.

Callan noticed my interest. "It's decrepit on purpose. It's the focus for the deterrent spell."

"A what?" I still couldn't comprehend that witches were also real. I added talking to a witch to my mental to-do list as well. I needed to find out more about the spell that was cast on me.

"A focus. I don't know much about witchcraft, but for big spells like this one, they use a focus to ground it. Any human that happens to make it this far out in the woods sees the sign for what it is, old and rundown, and the spell makes them move away from it. It keeps us from being discovered."

"So, shifters and witches get along?" I had no idea what any of the politics looked like, but generally, when there was more than one powerful side to be on, they fought.

"No. Witches take no sides; they only work for the highest bidder." His sneer told me exactly how he felt about that situation.

"Are there any other supernatural creatures I need to be worried about?" My mind raced through all the possibilities of what could exist. "Are vampires real too?"

A sly smile was his only answer. We walked out the gates and through a small parking lot, stopping in front of a black four-door jeep, windows tinted so dark I could only see my reflection. It was exactly the car I would have pegged him to drive. I got in, noticing the immaculate cleanliness of the vehicle.

We drove in uncomfortable silence, the forest whizzing past at the speed of light. Callan drove like a maniac, weaving in and out between cars just to get a few feet ahead. I white-knuckled the door handle, fearing for my life.

"Are you trying to kill me so you don't have to work with me anymore?" I choked out, forcing myself to keep my eyes open. If I was going to die, I wanted to see it coming.

His eyes stayed glued to the road. "If I crashed, you wouldn't die. You'd heal too fast. And I never crash." The confidence would have been sexy if he hadn't been talking about my life.

I took advantage of the silence to sort out my thoughts. I still had so many questions running through my head, things I needed to know. I hadn't even gotten a chance to explore this new part of me that I had only just experienced last night. I was a shifter, and I had turned into a rabbit. A freaking rabbit.

It wasn't the coolest animal out there, but I had felt so at home in that skin. The wind whipped past me as I bobbed and weaved through the shrubbery, which most people didn't even pay attention to. And now, in my human form, things looked different as well. Better. I even felt stronger. I remembered what Lily said about my human form having benefits, and I couldn't wait to learn more about that. I'd already noticed the sense of smell and speed. What else could there be?

I still didn't know these people, but they had helped me get this far, which had to count for something. I would stay, at least until I got the answers I was searching for. Right after we caught this bastard.

I studied Callan in my peripherals, unsure what to make of him. In some moments, he was helpful. But at other times, he was withdrawn, arrogant, and stubborn. I didn't know if I could trust him to watch my back if anything dangerous happened.

And why was he a rogue in the first place? Based on what the Supreme had said, it sounded a lot like he had killed someone. But surely, if he had done that, he wouldn't have been allowed to roam free. I needed to find out more about him, and if he was dangerous, I needed to know.

I rubbed my fingers over my eyes, suddenly tired. I could have been at the beach right now, sipping a mimosa or something.

Or a 99-cent soda because that was all I could afford, but still.

Chapter Eleven

By the time we pulled up to the side of the highway I had been attacked on, I was about ready to scream. Anytime I tried to make small talk or play music, Callan shut me down. It seemed like he was intent on stewing in his misery or whatever it was that made him the way he was.

Getting out of the car, I took in the sight of the accident. I don't know why I expected to be blocked off, with yellow tape everywhere and official people milling about. It looked the same as if nothing had ever happened. "What happened to my car?"

"Wolfe had it towed to the junkyard. It'd cost more to fix than it's worth," Callan replied. I nodded, I had figured as much, but it didn't stop the wave of emotion as it welled up inside me. SB had gotten me through a lot of tough times. I'd bought her with my own money the second I turned eighteen and was on my own, having had to save for years working after school to afford the dinosaur. She deserved better.

"Are you...crying?" There was an undertone of panic to his mystified tone, not knowing what to do. I quickly brushed the few tears that had leaked out, giving him a glower.

"I really loved that car," I sniffled.

He rolled his eyes before turning away from me, and I shot eye daggers at his back.

"What do you smell?" he asked with an expectant tone, turning into teacher mode.

I tilted my face up towards the air and sniffed, my nose assaulted by all the different scents present. I sneezed three times in succession, my nose overwhelmed.

"I smell everything," I stated, eyes watering from all the sneezing.

"Scenting for shifters is an art," he told me. "We scent in layers. If you concentrate hard enough, you should be able to pick each one apart, commit it to memory, and peel back the layers to isolate the smells. Once you've cataloged a smell in your brain, you'll have it forever. We don't forget scent."

My eyes widened in shock. "Never? There are so many things in the world. How is that possible?"

He shrugged. "Shifting is genetic, yes, but it's also magic. We are part human and part magic. That is what allows us to keep a human form and an animal form."

"So, we can also wield magic?" I could not keep the budding excitement out of my voice.

"No," he said with a dark chuckle. He didn't often laugh, the sound like a gentle caress, and I was pleased that I had been the cause. "But we have a variety of benefits depending on the animal. Some shifters have agility, speed, strength, hearing, and smell. It just depends."

"Which ones do you have?" He seemed to be in a sharing mood now, which was a direct contrast to how he had been earlier. I was just grateful he was telling me more about this world that I had been thrust into.

"All of them." He met my eyes, his emerald gaze boring into mine, and I felt the heat rise to my cheeks. I cleared my throat, breaking eye contact and turning towards some trees that lined the road. I discretely fanned my face, cursing my pale skin that always showed the slightest bit of heat. I did everything I could to not look at him.

A large oak tree stood before me, stretching up toward the sky. It stood out from the rest, a large splotch of blackish brown adorning the trunk. There was a matching patch of color on the grass below. My blood, I realized with a shiver. I approached, as if in a trance, kneeling on the ground in front of the tree. Breathing came heavier as I tried to remember what had happened.

"Close your eyes." Callan's voice startled me as he kneeled beside me, pulling me out of the spiral I was getting lost in. "Breathe deeply. Focus on what you smell, and your brain will start cataloging it. Once you feel comfortable, pull back the layers and search. Find what doesn't belong."

After a brief hesitation, I did, closing my eyes and taking a deep breath. My nose was immediately overwhelmed again, and I sneezed hard.

"Slowly, Rowan," he whispered softly in my ear. His voice soothed my frazzled nerves, a warmth spreading through me that had nothing to do with the weather. "Isolate the scents."

I concentrated harder, and with surprise, it worked. Each note was like a piece of paper, and once I recognized it, I was able to pull it back and file it away, moving on to the next one. I sat there for a long time, identifying and storing scents in my head. Callan stayed in his spot behind me, waiting patiently.

I learned there was a difference between humans and shifters in the way they smelled. Humans didn't smell very good, like a mix of sweat and mortality. Shifters, on the other hand, smelled like the earth. I could identify a few scents I now recognized as Wolfe, Callan, and Malachi, the beta I had met earlier in the mess hall. They all had the same earthy undertone that told me they were shifters.

I instinctively moved closer to the tree, touching my nose to my dried blood on the ground. Inhaling deeply, I searched and sorted, and it was there that I found one more scent buried deep. It was like it was trying to flee from me, but once I found it, I couldn't let it go. It was intoxicating, a mix of the earthy tones of a shifter coupled with hints of vanilla and jasmine.

"What did you find?" Callan interrupted, and I opened my eyes to meet his.

"I think I caught their scent," I told him, excitement building up inside of me. I was doing something helpful in this search, learning to use my new talents, and it was exhilarating.

"What does it smell like?" he asked, inhaling his nose towards the ground like I had been. I'm sure I looked ridiculous when I did it, but he managed to pull it off. I described the scent to him, and his brow furrowed as he breathed in again before looking up, something unreadable in his eyes.

"I don't smell that."

I dipped my head again, inhaling, and found it almost immediately. Now that I knew it was there, it was easy to lock on. It's right there," I said, pointing like he could see it before I put my hand down, feeling ridiculous.

"I can't smell it," he said again, clearly unhappy about it, a thunderous cloud of anger settling over him.

"What does that mean?" I asked.

"It means we need a witch. Someone is fucking with us."

Chapter Twelve

Before we could see a witch, Callan took me to the other two crime scenes to test his theory. At each one, I could smell it, an earthy shifter mixed with that intoxicating vanilla and jasmine scent. Callan, on the other hand, could not, becoming increasingly enraged by that fact. By the time we finished the last one in Seaville, I thought he might set the whole town on fire.

It was well into the night when we loaded back into the car towards the pack. Each town was a few hours away from the other, making a large triangular pattern with the Clover pack lands. I couldn't help but doze off, exhausted from the day's events, my nose almost numb. As the car jolted to a halt, I was startled awake and took in our surroundings. I turned to Callan in confusion as we pulled back up towards the rusted gates of Clover.

"Aren't we going see a witch?" I questioned hesitantly. I thought we had made some progress at the site of my accident, but since then, he'd returned to his withdrawn self, silently fuming.

"Not tonight," he replied, pulling the keys out of the ignition but making no move to get out. "Go get some sleep, and I'll set up a meeting. It'll be a couple of days."

"When?"

He shrugged. "Witches operate on their own time."

"Why do you think you can't smell it? Another spell?"

He met my gaze, eyes looking almost black in the darkness of the car, but he didn't say anything. I stared back, not willing to back down. Getting information from him was like pulling teeth. I crossed my arms over my chest, narrowing my eyes at him.

"I'm not getting out of this car until you tell me."

He glared back. "You'll get out of the car if I tell you to get out."

I rolled my eyes at him, barely containing the snarky laugh that threatened to escape me. "Your Alpha male bullshit won't work on me. I had to force you to let me come with you today. How do I know you won't set up the meeting and go without me?"

His brows shot up in surprise for a split second before he schooled his expression. "You'll just have to trust me."

This time I did laugh. "Trust you? Why would I trust you when I have to force everything out of you? Why are you so resistant to letting me help you?"

"Because I'm fine on my own," he said grimly, averting his eyes. My anger flared, and I leaned forward.

"This isn't just about you. I was attacked and almost died, and I don't know why. I want to catch the fucker responsible for this." I swallowed hard. It was true. It wasn't just about the money. "And there are two families out there, waiting for answers on why their children were taken from them."

He opened his mouth to respond, but I cut him off. "I don't know why you have this chip on your shoulder but get over yourself. Two heads are better than one, and you can't even catch the scent. You need me."

He was silent for a long moment, his gaze pinned to my face, studying me. I waited for him to yell at me, challenge me, but he didn't. He wasn't stupid, and he knew I was right.

Instead, he leaned forward, eyes locked on mine until I could almost feel his breath on my face. I felt the heat rise in my cheeks, but I didn't back down. He inhaled deeply, eyes closing. When he opened them a moment later, the intensity in his gaze made my breath catch.

"I don't need anyone." His voice was barely above a whisper, reverberating through the silent car. He leaned closer, and for a moment, I thought he might kiss me, as ludicrous as it seemed. The car door popped open, and I felt the sudden breeze of the cool night air as he opened my door and leaned back, all intensity gone now. "One week. Meet me here, 5 PM. I'll pick you up."

I watched him a second longer until I was satisfied he meant it, before I hopped out and trudged my way back to my house, thoughts swirling.

Why did Callan affect me so much? I'd been with some guys before, but my body had never reacted so strongly to anyone. It was like I was a horny teenager in the presence of a cute guy for the first time. Sure, the guy was nice to look at, but his personality left much to be desired—the entirety of it. And I didn't know anything about him.

There's only one way to fix that, I thought to myself.

THE WEEK WENT BY QUICKLY, AND I FELL INTO A steady rhythm in the pack. Wolfe ordered Lily and Evie to train me, and most of my days were spent with them in the courtyard where I'd held my first shift.

"Concentrate, Rowan," Lily instructed me one brisk morning as we stood in the clearing. My eyes were shut, forehead scrunched as I tried to concentrate on shifting. Since the full moon, I'd been unable to shift on command. The most I'd been able to produce was a thin layer of white downy fur on my arms, but it was gone within seconds.

"Why is this so hard?" A grunt of frustration escaped me when nothing happened. I flopped to the ground, dejected.

"This is totally normal, you know," Evie said from her perch on a nearby rock. "It often takes months to get a good grasp on shifting on command. The more full moons you experience, the easier it'll get. Don't rush it."

"I meet with Callan tomorrow," I complained. "It would be much more helpful if I could shift."

"You won't need to," Lily told me. "You'll be safe with Callan."

"Will I?" I threw back. "He doesn't say much."

"Give him time. He just likes to keep to himself."

"What's his deal? Why does he live on the outskirts like a pariah? And why does everyone look at him like that?" I asked her from my place on the floor.

"Get up! Stamina is also a big part of being a shifter. Time to run laps," Lily ordered instead of answering, changing the subject. I could see on her face that she knew exactly what was up with Callan but didn't want to tell me.

I WOKE UP THE NEXT DAY WITH A MISSION. OPERATION: Find out more about Callan.

I moseyed my way to the mess hall, hoping to find someone I knew, and was not disappointed. Lily and Evie sat at the usual corner table, chatting animatedly over breakfast. After piling my tray high with hashbrowns, bacon, sausage, and eggs, I made my way over. Now that I had shifted, I noticed I'd been eating a lot more to keep up with the changes to my body. They both greeted me with a smile.

"Good morning, sunshine!" Lily greeted me, her eyes sparking with mischief.

"Morning," Evie echoed, a matching expression on her face.

"Good morning." I sat down warily, my eyes darting between the two of them. "Why are you looking at me like that?"

"We're going shopping," they said in unison.

"Shopping? For what?"

"The mating party!" Evie enthused excitedly, practically bouncing out of her seat. "It will be tomorrow night, during the Mating Moon."

"A mating party? And what the heck is a Mating Moon?"

"It's a celebration. We hold the mating ceremonies with our packs, but then we all come together and have one big reception." Evie grinned she was clearly all about the mate stuff. "The Mating Moon is the most fertile time of the month for a shifter. It has an aphrodisiac effect."

"Oh," I said dejectedly. I wasn't a huge fan of the whole love at first sight thing, but it had been a long time since I'd had some fun. Chad had never wanted to go out and party. "That sounds fun, but I don't have any money for shopping." I gestured to one of the same two outfits I'd been washing and re-wearing all week.

Lily laughed. "Oh, please. It's on Wolfe. He said you can pick whatever you want."

"He's going to regret that," I grinned from ear to ear. I'd make his pockets hurt. It was the least he could do for roping me into this mess. He would rue the day he met Rowan Miller.

Remembering my plans with Callan, I said, "I just have to be back here by five to see the witch with Callan."

Evie waggled her brows at me and giggled.

"Seriously, it's not like that. I'm trying to catch a killer!" I protested, unable to stop the blush rising in my cheeks. Lily met my eyes knowingly.

"We'll make sure we have you back by four," she sang.

The ride to the mall was filled with laughter, and I really found myself enjoying the time I'd spent with the girls. I had never made many friends growing up, and this was uncharted territory for me. They had opened their arms wholeheartedly to me when I arrived, and it might just be something I could get used to.

The Clover Mall was small, with just a couple of department stores and small boutiques, with a mediocre food court with the usual fast-food haunts. We found ourselves in Macy's, looking at a rack of dresses that resembled something you'd wear to a nightclub in Vegas.

"Are you guys sure these are appropriate? Isn't this a wedding type of thing?" I asked, eyeing a short black slip dress on a rack we were looking through. The slit went so high up I'm sure my vagina would be on full display.

Evie and Lily shared a conspiratorial glance. "Shifters party a little differently. It's common for newly mated shifters to get a little hands-on as the night goes on."

My eyebrows rose towards the heavens as Evie smirked. "And the non-mated shifters too."

"So you DO have orgies? Aren't you a little young for that?" I directed my question at Evie, remembering she was only seventeen.

She snorted a laugh, "Shifters are very possessive; we do not do group sex."

"No one under eighteen is allowed to stay past dinner," Lily chimed in, and I breathed a sigh of relief at both answers. "But let me warn you. The Mating Moon mostly affects the mated pairs as it's the best time for them to conceive, but the unmated females do feel some runoff. You'll be extra in the mood, but nothing you can't control."

"Oooh!" Evie exclaimed before I could ask further questions, pulling a forest green contraption off the rack. She held it up to my body. "This would look bangin' on you. Try it on!"

I laughed, an edge of hysteria to my voice. "I am not putting that on. No way, Jose."

Lily grabbed the dress, twirling it around in a circle around me. "Fine, don't try it on. We're buying it for you anyways."

The determined look in her eye told me there would be no

arguing with her so I only shrugged. Just because she bought it didn't mean I'd wear it.

"We're going to be late. Hurry up," I urged them, looking nervously at the clock. We'd had too much fun and had lost track of time.

By the time we'd left the mall, the girls had each picked questionably sexy dresses. I was laden with bags, having replaced my entire wardrobe while we were there. Besides the dress, I found a floor-length black gown that was much more my style. I also invested in a couple of pairs of jeans, tank tops, a beautiful leather jacket, and a couple of other one-off pieces. I had already changed into them and finally felt like myself again. Thanks, Wolfe.

"So, what's the deal with Callan?" I slipped between the girl's gossip as Lily drove us back towards the Clover pack. It was abrupt, but I had the best chance of getting an answer when Lily couldn't run away from me. Lily silenced immediately while Evie looked between the two of us curiously.

Lily shot me a side-eyed look before turning her attention back to the road.

"I notice the way everyone looks at him when he's around. It's like they're mad at him. Or scared."

Her lips flattened into a thin line when I kept pushing. "It's not my story to tell, Rowan."

I threw my hands up in frustration, turning to her with a pleading look in my eye. "For me to be able to solve these murders, I need to know. If he's dangerous, don't you think I deserve to know that?"

"He's not dangerous," she said after a pregnant pause, an edge of sadness in her voice. "I'll tell you because I like you, but you didn't hear it from me, okay? Wolfe told me the story, and I'm not supposed to know. " I nodded my head emphatically. She met Evie's eyes in the rearview mirror until she nodded as well.

"Callan used to be the Alpha of the Clover pack." She took a deep breath as I fought to keep my jaw off the floor. Out of all the things I thought she would say, I wasn't expecting that. Broody menacing cat man as Alpha? But the more I thought about it, the more it made sense how he had his own special magic. "Until his mate went crazy."

The blows just kept coming. I tried not to dwell on my disappointment that Callan had a mate as I waited for Lily to continue. I could care less if he had a mate.

"He was a good Alpha, or so the rumors say. I wasn't in the pack then. But his mate was not. She constantly challenged him every step of the way. They fought all the time. And then she got pregnant." Lily glanced at me, and seeing I was hanging on to her every word, she kept going.

"The pack struggles when the Alpha struggles. When she got pregnant, they rekindled, and the pack was finally in harmony." Lily's voice was almost a whisper, and I leaned closer to hear her. "It was stillborn; it happens a lot with shifter babies. The pregnancies are hard on the body. She got mixed up with people she shouldn't have, using substances she shouldn't. And then she snapped."

Lily said nothing, so I spoke, thinking the story was over. I looked in the backseat at Evie, seeing she was just as engrossed in this tale as I was. "So, she's in an institution somewhere?"

Her bottom lip trembled slightly, a white-knuckled grip on the steering wheel. "She became obsessed with the idea that all shifters were evil and had to be eradicated. Callan had her under lock and key, figuring out what to do with her."

"Wolfe was his beta at the time. She waited until they were called away to the annual leadership summit in Montana and broke out."

I studied the set of Lily's face, the grimness in her eyes, and read between the lines.

"She killed someone."

Lily tightened her grip on the steering wheel. "She killed everyone. And when Callan got back, he killed her."

Chapter Thirteen

We drove the rest of the way in silence, my mind reeling, trying to digest the information I had learned. I knew Callan had a past, that much was obvious, but this was beyond anything I could have imagined. His surly attitude made so much more sense now.

Part of me was relieved. At least he wasn't dangerous. The other part of me felt for him. Not only did he lose his mate, the one supposedly made by fate to be his other half, but he also lost his pack. The people he was responsible for, all of them. Dead. And he had to kill his mate himself. My heart ached for the pain he must have felt, the guilt he must carry.

Lily pulled up to the gates, and I cursed as I looked at the time. Twenty minutes late. Callan leaned against his black jeep, looking every bit as godly as he always did. He glared at us, arms crossed as he impatiently waited, his boot-clad foot tapping away at the gravel below.

"Oh shit," Lily mumbled, her voice cutting through the heavy silence that permeated the air. I reached over, giving her hand a quick squeeze.

"Thank you for telling me," I said, keeping my voice low, not knowing how far his shifter hearing might reach. I didn't have that skill in my human form. I gave her a reassuring smile, not matching what I felt inside. I opened the truck door and hopped out, relishing the satisfying thud of my new boots. Louder, I said, "Can you put my stuff in the house for me? If I'm not back in a few hours, send a search party."

At Lily's nod of confirmation, I waved goodbye to both of them and trotted over to the angry man.

"Sorry I'm late." I scratched my head awkwardly, trying to appear calm and not like I had just learned his earth-shattering news. He glowered at me, opening the passenger side door before storming over to the driver's side and getting in, the engine rumbling to life under his command.

Apologies weren't my strong suit, but he could have just as easily left me and gone by himself, but he didn't. I owed him one. "I don't have a phone, and we lost track of time."

He cut me a glance but said nothing, his jaw clenched.

I exhaled through my nose forcefully, irritation sparking at me. I know I was late, but he could at least say something. I glanced at him as he drove, pity in my heart as I mulled over what Lily had told me. He caught me staring, his lips thinning into a single line with displeasure.

"They told you," he said flatly. He didn't ask a question, so I didn't answer him, instead crossing my arms to my chest and looking out the window as he drove. He didn't speak further, and we drove on in silence, the trees slowly fading away as we drove towards town until I couldn't take it anymore.

"I'm sorry for what happened to you," I said finally. "I know—"

"You don't know anything," he said gruffly. Even from the side, I could see the golden flecks glittering in his eyes.

"I don't," I agreed. "I couldn't begin to put myself in your shoes, but I can empathize. You lost the love of your life. And your family."

I didn't know if he saw the pack the same way that Wolfe did, but it seemed like a common shifter outlook, especially for an Alpha. Or former Alpha.

"I didn't lose the love of my life," he growled. "She betrayed me, and she paid the price. It was simple."

"Oh, that I can relate to." A dark cloud passed over me briefly as I thought about Chad and what I had walked into. Callan spared a glance at me, a questioning look in his eye.

"My boyfriend." Something in Callan's gaze darkened, and I quickly corrected myself. "Well, my ex-boyfriend. It's not nearly on the magnitude of yours, but he betrayed me. I walked in on him in my bed with another woman."

"Did you kill him?"

I frowned back at him. Did he think normal people just went around killing people who betrayed them? "No, but I broke his nose."

His grin was feral as he looked over at me.

"Good."

WE PULLED UP TO A RED BRICK BUILDING OF A NORMAL-looking shopping outlet. Six different stores lined the outside, and my eye settled on one towards the far end, purple and gold lettering spelled out Second Chanted. Cute decals of witches' hats, cauldrons, and copious amounts of silver sparkles decorated the windows.

"The witches run magic shops?" It seemed entirely ridiculous to me.

"Some of them like to hide in plain sight," Callan answered as we approached. Our conversation in the car had eased some of the animosity between us, and I was grateful for it. Little by little, I was chipping away at his walls.

The inside of the shop was small but fully lit, every inch of space covered with various objects. I stopped walking in awe as I looked around. Sturdy black shelves covered every inch of wall space, filled to the brim with ornate-looking texts. The rest of the room was filled with odds and ends; herbs and flowers of all kinds, cauldrons, and glass vials covering every surface. I approached the bookshelf closest to me, running my fingers over the spines as I read the titles.

The Pocket Spellbook, Healing Hands for Dummies, How I Became a Potions Prodigy

The books went on for miles, stretching around the entirety of the store. No two books were the same. I entertained the thought of what it might be like to read these, to learn to wield magic. How freaking cool would that be?

"Rowan!" Callan hissed, and I shook myself out of my reverie. Turning back sheepishly, I realized he was standing at a counter with an old-fashioned cash register sitting on top, speaking to someone. I walked over, taking in the man standing behind it.

He was not much taller than me, his salt and pepper hair patchy on his balding head but thick on the bushy beard that clung to his chin. Big brown eyes looked out at me, a kindness to them that couldn't be faked. His eyes crinkled at the edges as he gave me a warm smile that I couldn't help but return.

"Rowan, is it?" He spoke with a slightly European-sounding accent that I couldn't quite place.

"That's my name, don't wear it out." He let out a boisterous laugh that I didn't expect, and I immediately knew I liked this guy.

Callan rolled his eyes, managing to still look good as he did it. The bastard. He slammed a heavy-handed paw on the counter. "We need information, witch."

The witch narrowed his eyes at Callan, suddenly looking less friendly. An alien power built in the air, much different from the Alpha power I had previously experienced. The hair on my arms stood on end, and I bolted forward, afraid of what a firefight between these two would do.

"What my friend here was so rudely trying to say," I cut Callan a glare before turning my most charming smile back to the witch, "Is that we would appreciate your help with something."

A beat passed, the witch looking between us, before I felt the charge in the air relax, dissipating into nothing after a few moments.

"I'd be happy to help a nice young lady like yourself." He made a point to only look at me, disregarding Callan entirely. "For the right price, of course."

"Price?" I figured he'd help us out of the goodness of his heart, but that had been naïve. Of course, he'd want something in return.

"Did you bring money?" I directed it toward Callan because I sure as hell didn't.

The shopkeeper laughed again. "I do not take payment in money, dear. I take payment in blood." My brows shot up in shock.

"Just make it quick." Callan sighed heavily, extending his right wrist towards the witch. My eyes widened as I stared at him in disbelief.

The man smiled, this one much more sinister than the first he had bestowed on me. He was not as innocent as he had first appeared. He reached forward, but instead of gripping Callan's wrist as I expected, he instead reached out with a firm grip and took mine. Lightning quick, he lowered his face to the lily-white skin of my wrist, inhaling deeply. Callan growled deep in his chest, sending goosebumps over my body as he lunged forward next to me.

"Be still, panther." He cut a glance at Callan, the strange crackling power building back up. It raced up and down my skin, small pinpricks of energy coursing over me, but it did not hurt me. I looked to Callan, who stood frozen in place, an angry snarl twisting his handsome features. The witch turned to look at me. "I will take my payment from you, or I will not help here."

"Why me?" I whispered softly. I wondered if Callan could still hear us in his magicked state.

He looked into my eyes, and I could almost see the deep well of power that lived inside of him. I got the impression that this man could kill both of us with no warning if he chose. I had no idea witches could be so powerful, but I wasn't scared of this man for some odd reason. I didn't trust him, but I didn't fear him either.

"There is something different about you, Rowan. Haven't you noticed it yet?"

"I don't know what you're talking about," I told him hesitantly. "I'm just a shifter—a rabbit at that. I'm not even a big scary animal like a panther. He's going to eat you when you release him." I cut my eyes towards Callan, still stuck in the same position.

The witch's eyes twinkled with delight. "He couldn't eat me if he tried."

"Can you tell me who cast a spell on me?" I questioned, figuring I might as well try to get some information from him. "They had to break it to allow me to shift for the first time."

"I can." Hope blossomed in my chest, and finally, someone who could give me the answers I sought. "There are a lot of things I can tell you. It's very impressive that your shifters could break through that. I sense powerful magic did this to you."

"Wait, you still sense it?" He grinned at me, revealing slightly stained yellowing teeth.

"Well, of course. He only broke one of them."

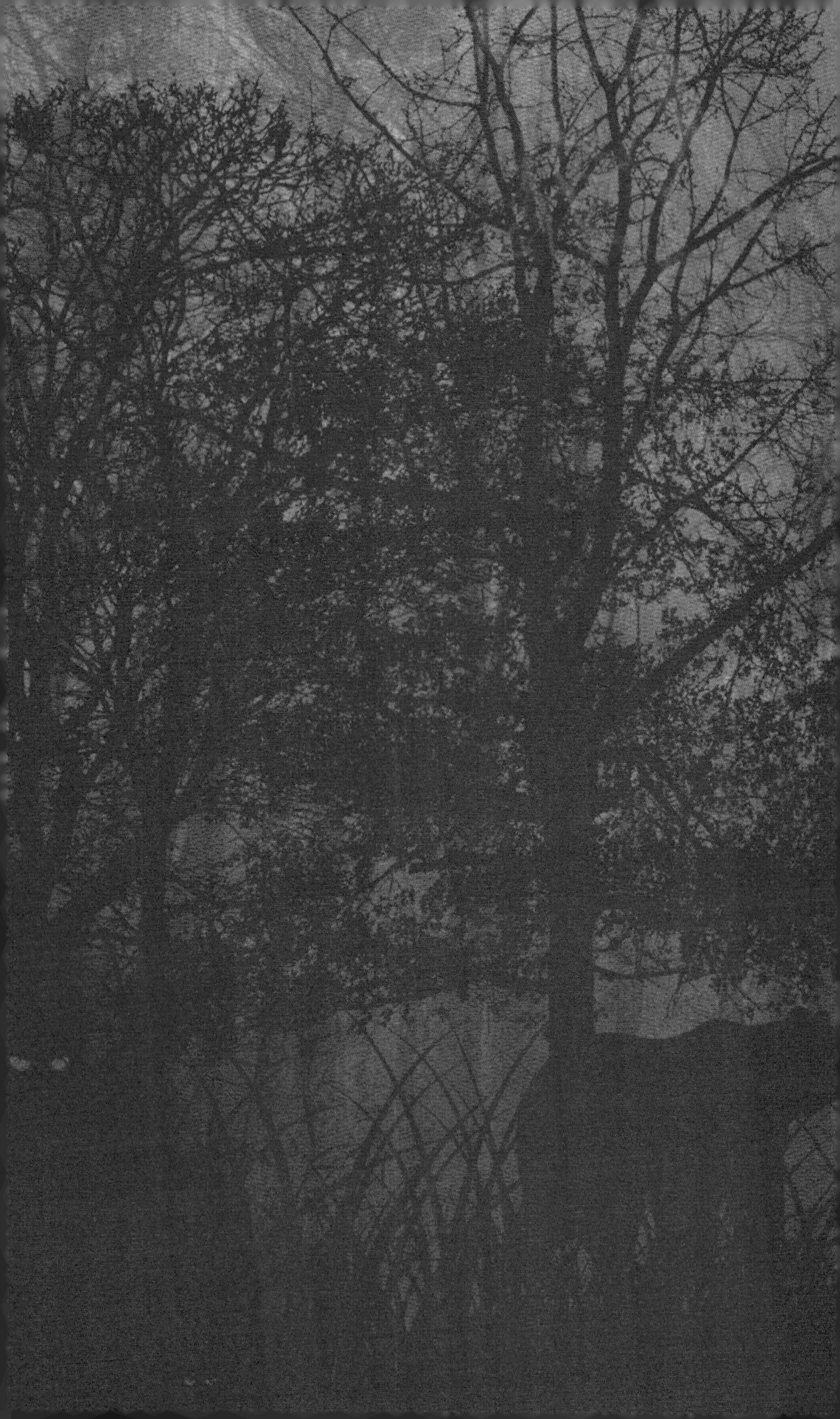

Chapter Fourteen

"One of them?"

"I sense multiple spells on you, my darling. At least two, maybe more."

I blinked at him. "Oh, okay, I get it. This is some scam, right? You pretend I'm cursed and convince me to give you my blood so you can do god knows what with it. And by the end, you won't even give us any information."

The witch's eyes sharpened, fixed on my face. "The reason your bodyguard here can't smell the murderer you seek is because they were spelled. Someone doesn't want the shifters to be able to smell them."

"Then why can I smell it?" It made no sense. I had barely even learned to use my nose. There should be no reason that I'd be able to smell through a spell if Callan and Wolfe, of all people, couldn't.

He barred his teeth at me in a semblance of a grin, gesturing to my wrist that he still held. I leveled my eyes at him, thinking through all my options before I resigned myself to my fate. I had to know the answers, and he was the only one who could provide them.

"I give you permission." I was happy when my voice didn't

waver, sounding much more confident than I felt. I hoped this didn't end in a mistake.

The witch smiled widely, reaching under the counter to pull out a small knife with a simple golden hilt, words I didn't recognize carved into the face of the blade. His grip tightened on my wrist as he slashed across it, and I gasped at the sudden pain.

I expected him to pull out a vial to catch the blood as it dripped down my wrist, staining the counter below, but he only swiped both sides of the blade in it until it was entirely coated in red. He muttered something intelligible under his breath, and I marveled as the blade glowed a soft golden hue, heat radiating from it. The glow faded with a sudden flash of light, and the blade looked exactly as it had before. My wrist itched as my shifter healing kicked in, quickly sealing the cut. In a few minutes, it would be like it never happened.

"That's it?" I was not comforted by the fact that he had sucked my blood up into his magical blade. The feeling that I had made a mistake increased tenfold. The witch ignored my question, tenderly tucking the knife back into its home under the counter.

"Will you answer my questions now?" I grew impatient. I'd held up my end of the deal. Now it was his turn.

"We should wake your friend up first. He grows restless under my spell, and I suspect he will break free soon." I wouldn't argue with that. This was Callan's hunt too, and he deserved to be privy to the information. He would be livid when he found out I gave my blood, but regardless, I nodded to the witch to continue. I could handle him.

"Wake, panther," he said softly, and Callan roared back to life. His eyes were molten gold as he looked between me and the witch, his dark power seeping from him in icy waves. He stalked towards the counter, teeth bared as he stepped in front of me protectively.

"What the fuck did you do? I smell blood." The witch straightened to his full height, nowhere close to matching Callan's towering figure but somehow just as intimidating. I swear, all I did was break up men and their pissing contests.

Reaching up, I placed my hand on Callan's arm. Ignoring the surge of heat that rushed through me at the feel of his muscled arm beneath mine, I pulled him towards me, forcing him to turn and face me. I felt his power dissipate slowly as he looked me up and down, searching for injuries he couldn't find.

"I paid the blood tax," I told him firmly, leaving no room for argument. I was an adult, and I could make my own damn decisions. "He will tell us what we want to know."

"You shouldn't have done that." His tone was grim, resigned. Now his power had completely calmed, only the chill of the shop AC permeating the air.

"I did what I had to. Now let's get some answers from... what's your name anyways?" I dropped Callan's arm, turning my attention back towards the witch. I can't believe I let him take my blood without knowing his name. Stupid.

"Oliver, at your service." He bowed deeply.

Callan glared coldly, still not happy about me paying his price. "You're lucky I don't rip your throat out where you stand, taking her blood before she understood the risks. Why can no one smell the perpetrator but her?"

"Someone has cast a spell on your culprit. They do not want to be found."

"That much is obvious. Stop wasting my time. Why can she smell them?"

"An educated guess? She was not a shifter at the time the spell was cast. The spell placed on her overshadowed this one, and when you broke through it, you enabled her to catch the scent."

"Wouldn't the spell caster have accounted for that?" I mused. I knew nothing about witchcraft, but it seemed sloppy that they wouldn't have made a stronger spell. "Seems like a shitty witch if you ask me."

Oliver laughed softly. "You are a funny one, child. That is not how witchcraft works, I'm afraid. Spells can interfere with other spells all the time."

"So, how do we track them down?" Callan was not in the mood for chitchat, the always-working muscle in his jaw twitching.

"I can create a tracking spell using the blood I collected. But I will need two things from you first. I need something with the scent on it that interacted with the culprit."

"I thought you might say that." Callan reached into his back pocket, pulling out a small Ziploc bag with something thin inside. Squinting at it as he placed it on the counter, I realized it was a sliver of bark, stained from my blood when I had hit it during my attack.

Oliver looked at the offering with surprise, clearly impressed. "You are familiar with spellcraft?"

Callan shrugged slightly, his eyes expressionless but offered no explanation. Oliver studied him briefly before picking up the bag and stowing it under the counter.

"You said two things?" I questioned.

"Time. Tracking spells are difficult, and it will take me time to gather everything needed. Give me one week. I will need Rowan with me when we cast it. Her connection to the caster will strengthen the potency."

"And that will lead us to this bastard?" Callan's voice was barely above a growl, his excitement at being near the end of this hunt palpable.

Oliver didn't hesitate. "No. But I can lead you to the witch who cast the spell."

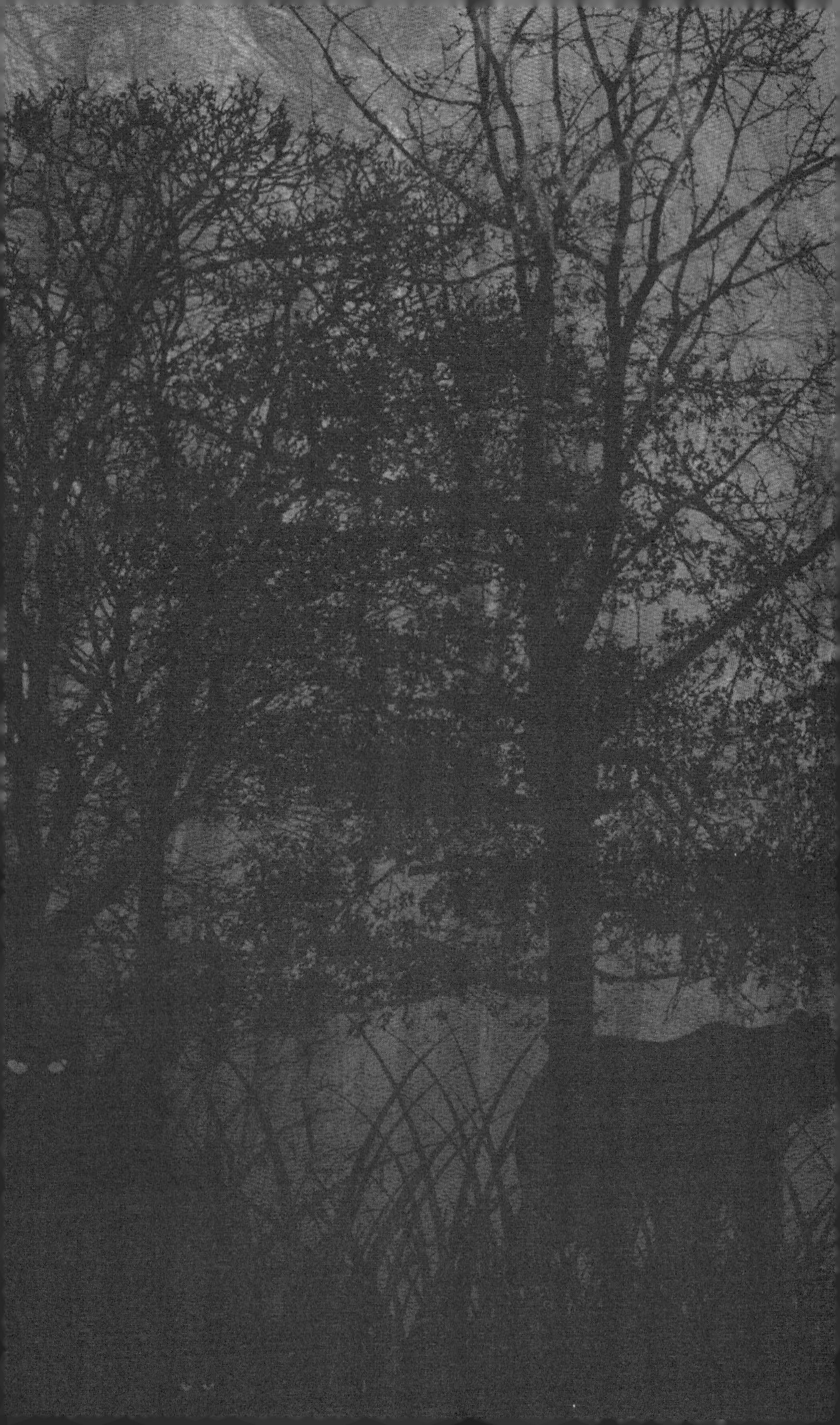

Chapter Fifteen

We exited the shop shortly after, heading back towards the car.

"Start the car. I'll be there in a minute." Callan handed me the keys and, without waiting for an answer, turned and headed into the general store next to the magic shop. I debated disobeying the order; I hated being ordered around but decided against it. We'd finally gotten to some semblance of a partnership, and I didn't want to poke the bear. Or the cat, in this case.

Sliding into the passenger seat, I coaxed the engine to life, stewing in my thoughts. I admired my wrist, the crusted blood the only sign that there had ever been an injury in the first place. Even though I knew I was a shifter now, it never failed to surprise me when my new talents showed up.

Reminded of my new revelation, I reflected on the witch's words. The fact that there were more spells shocked me. I could access my rabbit form and extra abilities like healing and sense of smell. What more could the spells be hiding? And who had put them on me in the first place?

I never knew who my parents were. Social services tried to find a parent, but they never could, and pretty soon, I was lost in the shuffle of the system. I never thought I was anything but ordinary.

I needed more information from Oliver, but I hadn't wanted Callan to overhear. While we had come to a tentative truce, I still wasn't sure how much I could truly trust him. What if there was a deeper reason there were more spells on me? What if it was something someone could use against me? I knew nothing about this world. I vowed to get Oliver alone the next time we met and figure out how to break the rest of the spells. For better or for worse, I wanted to be entirely myself. No magical interference, not anymore.

My thoughts catapulted to the present as the car door popped open. Callan slid in, tossing a white plastic bag in my lap. After a brief hesitation, I opened it, a smile erupting across my face when I saw the contents.

"You bought me a cell phone?" The bag held one of the newest phone models, a charger, and a case.

"I need to be able to contact you. My number is already programmed in there. No need to pay me back." The car jerked over a speed bump as he backed it up and steered us onto the main road.

"Are you feeling okay?" His sideways frown made me laugh out loud. "I didn't think you were capable of being this nice."

I was only mostly joking.

"You could just say thank you," he said dryly.

I bit back my usual rapid-fire retort. As much as I'd love to sass him, he had done a very nice thing.

"Thank you!" I exclaimed instead, already clicking away through the different screens, exploring my new gadget. It was leagues nicer than the phone I had before. Minutes passed in silence as the landscape blurred alongside us.

"Wolfe wants to see us when we get back. He wants a status update." Callan spoke into the quiet, sounding none too happy about it.

"Do you hate Wolfe? For taking your job?"

The silence stretched so long I wasn't sure he'd reply, but then he said, "He didn't take my job. I chose to become a rogue. I could have fought to stay as Alpha if I wanted to."

"Why didn't you? Couldn't you have rebuilt the pack with Wolfe and started over?" I was pushing my luck, but I was nothing if not nosey as hell.

He gave me a pointed look. "I failed my pack. I don't deserve to have a new one."

The thinly veiled pain in his voice broke my heart. He'd forced himself to live on the outskirts on purpose, perpetually punishing himself for something he didn't even do.

"But it wasn't your fault," I protested. He hadn't murdered his pack. That had been his mate.

"It's the Alpha's responsibility to keep their pack safe. I left them vulnerable to attack, and by their Alpha female no less. I should have been there; I should have seen it coming. I will spend the rest of my life repenting for my mistake." The seriousness in his green eyes shone through.

I reached over, placing a comforting hand on his shoulder. His shoulder jumped, startled that I'd touched him, and I half expected him to shrug it off, but he didn't.

"Don't let someone else's mistake stop you from living your life. You're allowed to move on." He said nothing, eyes focused on the drive ahead, and I dropped my hand back into my lap. That he hadn't bit my head off was a good sign, but I hated that he blamed himself.

It wasn't long before we reached the rusted gate of the pack lands. Instead of stopping at the gates like usual, Callan drove us through the compound and parked in front of Wolfe's log mansion instead. Wolfe threw open the door as we approached, his shifter hearing no doubt alerting him to our presence long before we saw him.

"Hello, gorgeous," Wolfe greeted me with a charming smile, nostrils flaring as he took in my scent. A low rumble sounded behind me, and I turned, only to see Callan, who met my eyes with a bored expression. Wolfe laughed softly under his breath, and I refocused my attention on him.

"I like the new look." His grey eyes twinkled as he looked me up and down. "It looks good on you."

"I'll look even better when I get the ten thousand you promised." I grinned innocently back at him, meeting his eyes. I was beginning to think Wolfe flirted with everyone, and I was not the type of girl to get caught up in his stride.

Callan pushed past me gruffly as Wolfe chuckled, leading us down a hallway toward a large living room. It surprised me that Callan knew his way around until I realized this was probably his house when he was Alpha. Depressing.

A black leather sectional was the only furniture to sit on, looking miniature in such a large room. A flat-screen TV mounted the wall, and a matching black coffee table sat in front of the couch, littered with various papers and magazines.

"You are in sore need of an interior decorator," I told Wolfe as we sat on the sofa, unable to hold my tongue any longer. "You'll never find a mate at this rate."

Wolfe threw his head back and laughed, deep and throaty. "That's the beauty of being a shifter, Ro. My mate will be stuck with me whether I decorate my house or not."

I rolled my eyes at him. God help the woman who gets mated to this man. "In all seriousness, thank you for the clothes. I was missing the closet I left behind, and I was able to replace most of it."

"Always happy to spoil a pretty lady," he replied with a wink.

"Can we get on with it already?" Callan ground out, his jaw clenched. Wolfe gave him a sly look before turning serious.

"Where are you at with the investigation? The Alpha Supreme wants an update."

"You can tell your dad," Callan emphasized the last word, a triumphant gleam in his eye when Wolfe flinched. "That we have a lead. The shifter responsible for this is spelled, but we've found a witch to track the caster for us."

"Spelled?" Wolfe nodded as he mulled this over, the puzzle pieces clicking into place behind his eyes. "That makes a lot of sense. Were you able to scent the attacker?"

I nodded. "I caught the scent at the site of my accident and found it at each crime scene we went to. Oliver says he needs a week to be ready to cast the tracking spell."

"Oliver, the witch?"

"Yes." I did not mention the other information he had told me about the spells on myself. That was an issue for another day. "You know him?"

"He's built a reputation for himself. You paid him already?" Wolfe directed the question towards Callan, who shot me a dark look.

"I would have if he hadn't cast a freeze spell on me and taken it from this idiot instead."

"You did WHAT?" Wolfe's roar of outrage surprised me since he normally seemed so even-tempered. I shrugged, trying to appear as nonchalant as possible. "It was no big deal."

"It's a huge deal, Rowan." Wolfe let out a heavy breath. "A witch can use a shifter's blood for many things. Occult blood increases the potency of spells, enabling the user to cast much stronger spells than they normally would be able to."

"That's not such a bad thing then, is it? Wouldn't that make the tracking spell that much stronger?"

"And the next dozen spells after that," Callan deadpanned. My eyes widened, realization setting in.

"There are so many unknowns when it comes to you. You should have let Callan pay the price. We don't know what effect your blood will have when mixed with magic."

"I'm a shifter." It felt good to say those words. I hadn't realized until now I'd never said it out loud. "My blood should have the same effect as yours."

Wolfe leaned closer to me, eyes closing briefly as he breathed in my scent. Callan stiffened rigidly from his spot on the couch beside me, and he leaned forward, almost protectively. "I think we all know you're not just a shifter."

Before I could say anything else, Wolfe clapped his hands together and stood up. "I'll be joining you for the tracking spell. The witch that is hiding this bastard isn't going to want to come quietly. You will need backup. We'll take a team."

Callan growled, low in his throat. "Rowan and I will get all the information we need."

It was silly, but happiness surged through me at his words. He was finally thinking of me as his partner, not just the deadweight he had to drag along.

"I wasn't asking," Wolfe replied flatly. "Someone is preying on innocent shifters, and, as Alpha, it's my responsibility to protect my pack. It takes a witch of high caliber to create a spell of this size. You, of all people, should understand that."

Callan's glare turned to ice as I felt the familiar creep of his power next to me. Standing quickly, I stepped in front of him, blocking the line of sight on both sides. That was a low blow, and I did not want to clean any blood off my new clothes so soon. "Are we done here? I have clothes to unpack and a dress to iron before the party tomorrow."

"The mating party?" Callan asked cautiously, his expression unreadable. At my nod, he turned to look at Wolfe. "Do you think that's wise? She should stay home."

I stamped my foot on the ground indignantly. "Excuse you. I'm a grown-ass woman. I'll go to a party if I feel like it."

"You don't understand," he tried, but I cut him off, whirling around to point a finger in his face.

"No, I understand completely. It's been a long time since I've been able to let loose and have some fun, and I'm not letting you stop me. I'll see you in a week."

With that, I turned on my heel and stormed out of the house, slamming the door shut behind me.

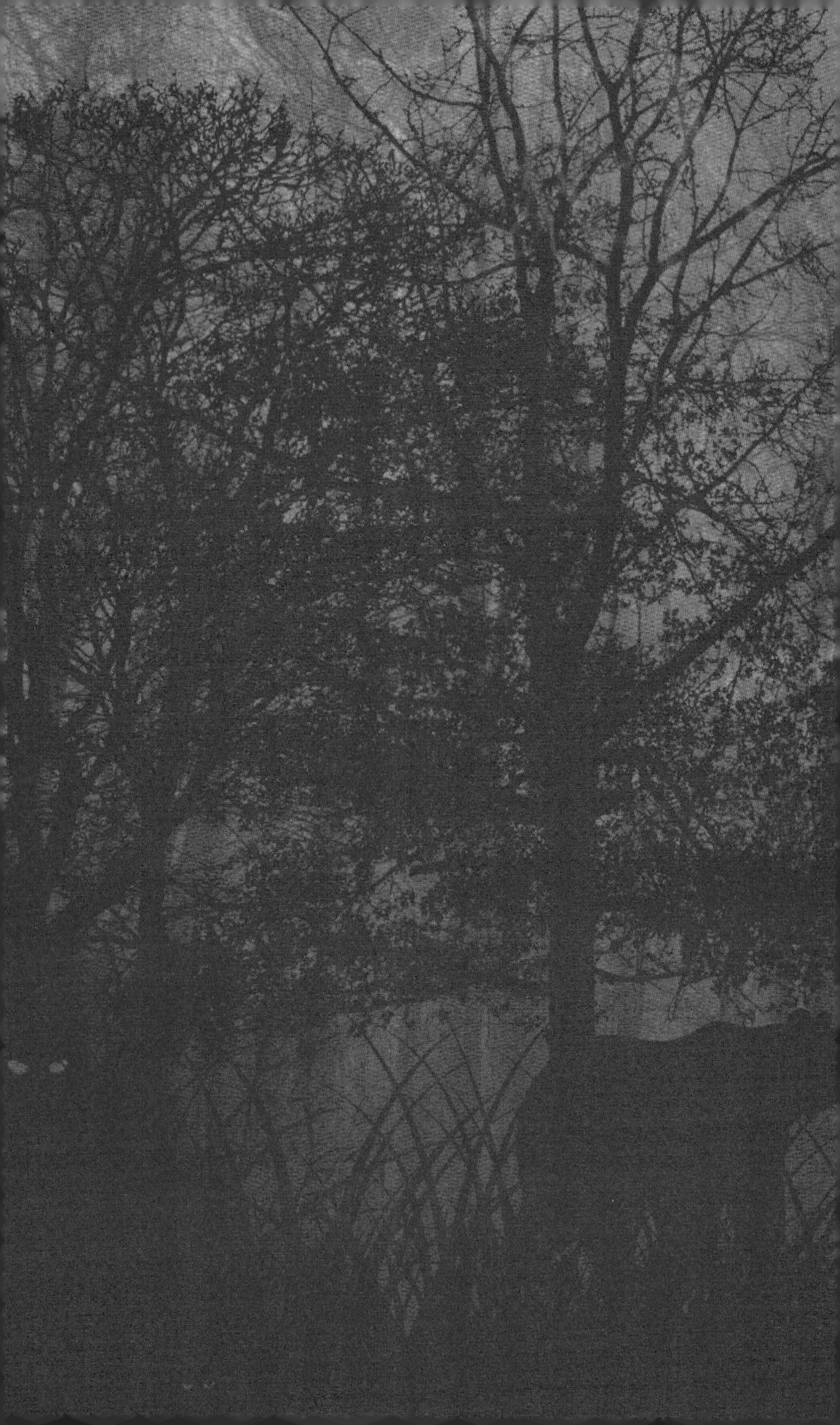

Chapter Sixteen

"Come for me."

Callan's voice was like velvet in my ear, the hot whisper of his breath brushed against my skin as he thrust into me with unrelenting force. I quivered under him, walls squeezing against his cock as he pounded into me. I met his every thrust, chasing the release I so desperately needed.

I reached a hand towards his head, trying to pull his lips down to meet mine, aching for intimacy. Instead, he gripped my arms, pinning them above my head on the bed. My anger sparked at the denial even as the pressure inside me continued to build.

"Come," he commanded again, breathing hard. I strained against his hold, trying to break my hands free so I could touch him, to no avail.

"Fuck you," I moaned at him, and he chuckled.

"The only one getting fucked here is you," he told me before releasing one hand, reaching down to circle my clit deftly with his fingers. The bed slammed against the wall with the force of his thrusts. All rational thought left my mind as my orgasm built, dancing just out of reach. Just a little more.

"Maybe if you asked nicely," I egged him on, my hips gyrating against him uncontrollably, rocketing towards a climax I knew would break me.

His breath was hot as he lowered his face next to mine, the harsh pants he let out with each plunge hotter than anything I'd ever heard. His lips tickled as he placed a scorching kiss on my neck before putting them right next to my ear.

"Please, Rowan."

I screamed, hips bucking as I-

My bedroom door slammed open, startling me awake. Lily and Evie barged in; concern written on their faces.

"Are you okay? We heard screaming, and we-"Evie trailed off as she took in the sight of the room, nostrils flaring. I panted on the bed, chest heaving as I fought off the remnants of my dreamy arousal, trying not to dwell on the disappointment of not finishing it. I really needed to put a lock on my cabin.

Lily grinned as she gripped Evie's arm, slowly backing out of the room. "We'll, uh, leave you to it. Hop in the shower. It's time to get ready for the party. You overslept!"

With that, they left the room, the quiet click of the door the only sound they made as they exited. I dissolved into the sheets, breathing still heavy from my dream. If I fell back asleep, would I be able to pick up where I left off?

Get a grip! It was Callan we were talking about here. Brooding, sometimes nice, but mostly infuriating Callan. Who had already had his chance with his true mate. Even if I did want him, which I didn't, I could never be his mate. No one could.

I took a few more moments to gather myself before I hopped in to take a shower that could only be rivaled by a dip in the Arctic. I stayed there for way longer than necessary, finally feeling my heart rate return to normal. A pit of heat stayed in my belly, but there was nothing I could do about that right now. I had a party to get ready for.

I exited my room wearing a knee-length t-shirt, my hair wrapped in a towel. I smiled as I watched the girls in my living room, the tv playing reruns of a sitcom as Lily applied makeup to Evie's face.

"I'd ask if you slept well, but I think we all know how that went." They erupted in peals of laughter at Lily's joke, and I felt my cheeks burn hot.

"Hey, a girl has needs. Not much action to get around here, I'm afraid."

Lily gave me a knowing look. "I hear you on that. Maybe you'll meet a nice shifter guy at the party tonight? I bet Wolfe would take you up on the offer. He seems to be sweet on you."

"I think Wolfe might be sweet on everyone," I scoffed. Wolfe was not on my to-do list. Don't get me wrong, he was hot, but jumping into bed with the Alpha would be a terrible idea. Especially when we already knew we weren't mated, having met in animal form during my first shift.

Lily laughed, "He is a bit of a flirt. A lot of us have fallen into his trap before."

I didn't miss her words, brows raising in surprise. "You had sex with Wolfe?"

"We dated once upon a time." She looked down wistfully for a moment. "But we both knew it couldn't last. We weren't mates, so we cut it off. Years ago."

My expression softened as I observed the sadness in her voice. "Couldn't you still be together anyways? Just say fuck you to the mates?"

She looked flabbergasted. "Absolutely not. When you meet your true mate, it's all-consuming. They say it's like finding the missing half of your soul. It would have been irresponsible for us to carry on, knowing that eventually, one of us would get hurt when we found a mate."

"And you always know when you meet in animal form?" she nodded.

"The bond flares to life when you see each other for the first time and then is locked in when the mating ceremony is performed." Lily returned to Evie's makeup, dusting a dark powder across her cheeks to make them look sharper.

"And you only have one mate?" I tried to be nonchalant, not wanting her to catch on to the true reason for my question. I let out a relieved breath when she answered, still focused on Evie.

"Yes. If one mate dies, often the other one does too. Not always, but most of the time. The ones that manage to live will never mate again. Never. I would not want to live in a world without my mate." She shivered at the thought.

I blinked against the disappointment I felt. I had already guessed that there was only one mate per person, and I was certainly not in love with Callan, so I wasn't sure why I cared so much that he'd never have another one. I needed to let whatever irrational attraction I had for him go and get on with my life. This confirmation only cemented that fact.

"Can you do my makeup too?" I asked Lily with a smile, changing the subject.

"Already planning on it!"

THREE HOURS LATER, MY FACE AND HAIR HAD BEEN thoroughly beaten into submission.

"What do you think?" I turned to the girls, the black floor-length gown I had purchased at the mall draping my figure. They scrunched up their noses as they looked at me and then at each other.

"Honest opinion?" Evie asked hesitantly.

"Obviously."

"You look like you're going to chaperone the prom," she deadpanned, and Lily snickered before my glare shut her up.

"I do not!" I argued, even though in the back of my mind, I agreed. This dress had looked much better on the rack than it did on me now. Lily stared at me expectantly, wearing down my resolve. "Ugh, okay, you're right. This is somebody's mom's dress."

"Good thing we bought two options!" Lily singsonged as she walked to my closet, pulling out the garment bag I had shoved to the very back. Seeing my mouth open to protest, she cut me off before I got the chance.

"Just humor us. If you hate it, I'll get you a dress from my closet." I frowned at her, but when she shook the dress in my face, I reluctantly took it. The faster I tried it on, the faster she'd give me something else to wear once she saw how terrible I looked.

I quickly changed in the bathroom, pulled the dress into place, and turned to look in the floor-length mirror that leaned against one wall. I audibly gasped at my reflection, seeing my face for the first time since we'd started getting ready.

Lily had done a sultry smokey eye on me, my lips painted with a deep red color that I had never thought I could pull off. Evie had proved to be a wizard with a curling iron, my long blonde locks cascading around my face in perfectly tousled waves. A natural flush was in my cheeks, the heat from my earlier dream still ever-present.

The dress itself was a deep forest green, rich and luxurious. The straps hung slightly off the shoulder, a delicate lace floral pattern etched across the bodice. It was also floor length but with a questionably high slit on one side, and I knew if I made the wrong move, I'd be putting on a show for more than just my dreams tonight. The neckline was deep and dipped down suggestively, and I thanked the stars that I had remembered to grab a push-up bra at the mall. I didn't have much going on up there, but in this dress, it sure looked like I did.

The fabric clung to my curves in all the right places, and looking in the mirror, I looked like a goddess. I couldn't even deny it. This dress was made for me. I wonder what Callan would say about this dress; the intrusive thought escaped me before I could tamp it down. Shaking my head at my clearly hormonal self, I fluffed my hair, ensuring it looked just right. Using a quick spritz of lavender body spray, I left the bathroom and returned to the girls, giving them a sheepish look as I presented myself.

"Holy fuck, Rowan. You look HOT!" Evie gawked as she looked at me, and I laughed.

"I hate admitting when I'm wrong, but...this dress is it. I'm sorry I doubted you, Queen Lily. Judging by how stunning you both look, I should have known you were right."

They had changed while I was in the bathroom, and I was equally in awe of their beauty. Evie looked innocently effortless in a deep purple gown, stopping just above knee high with a corseted top. Her strawberry blonde hair was pulled up into a matching butterfly clip, her makeup accentuating her big brown eyes.

Lily was a vision in red, her tanned skin the perfect complement to her dress. Side cutouts highlighted her wide hips and tiny waist. Many women would have paid to look as good as she did, and she knew it.

Lily threw an arm around our shoulders, guiding us to the door. "The boys are going to lose their minds over us. Evie, I trust you'll make yourself scarce after dinner?" She looked at her pointedly, and I remembered that Evie was not allowed to attend the party.

"Yes, Mom," she whined dejectedly. Lily did keep a motherly eye on Evie since she had none, even if they were also friends. Lily had a big heart; that much was obvious.

"Then let's get this party started!"

Chapter Seventeen

The festivities were in full swing as we walked towards the town center, the sun just starting to set on the horizon. Dozens of people mingled about, and I could feel the buzz of excitement in the air.

"Six couples were mated in the ceremonies today." Lily beamed with pride. "None from our pack, but that's okay. The more mated couples we find, the better. Six is a huge number."

"Are there not a lot of couples that are mated?" I'd met only a couple of mate pairs living in the Clover pack, but most of the shifters I'd seen were single.

"It's very hard to find a mate for most. Shifters live all over the world, in many packs across the globe. For all I know, my mate could be somewhere in Africa."

"So when a mate bond is found, we celebrate!" Evie said joyously. Their excitement for the mate bonds was beginning to grow on me. Even if I didn't think it would happen for me, I was happy for these couples that had found their other half.

We made the rounds, Lily and Evie introducing me to shifters of all kinds. I received more than a few appraising looks from the men we met, heat in their gaze, and I felt more confident with every step.

It struck me then that I didn't see anyone over thirty, many I would have pegged as mid-twenties.

"Where are the old people?" I asked callously. The oldest shifter I'd seen so far had been the Supreme Alpha, but he hadn't looked a day over forty.

"Once we hit twenty, our aging slows drastically," Lily said bluntly.

"How slowly?" I was scared to hear the answer. It hadn't struck me that there was increased longevity as a shifter.

"It takes about 100 years to get to forty. And after that, it stops completely." My eyes bugged out of my head as I took that in. I was going to live indefinitely?

"How old is the Supreme Alpha?"

"200, I think?" She squinted her eyes in concentration before lifting one shoulder in a shrug. "We stop keeping count. Age is just a number as far as we're concerned. When we get to a certain age, usually around the 300 mark, we have a tendency to go crazy and need to be put down."

"He had Wolfe when he was really old?" Lily shook her head.

"Shifters can only produce children for the first 50 years after finding their mate. Before that, we're completely infertile."

"So that means Wolfe is-" I wracked my brain, trying to compete in the mental Olympics for math.

"Wolfe is what?" A cheery voice sounded from behind me, and I whirled around, face to face with the man himself. He looked dashing in a classic black tux with a matching bowtie.

"How old are you?" I blurted out.

"Not a day over seventy-five," he replied with a wink, no hesitation whatsoever. He could have been joking, but the sincerity in his eyes said he wasn't. My breath whooshed out from me, speechless.

"Holy shit."

Wolfe smirked at me, amusement dancing in his grey eyes. "You still have a lot to learn about this life. It would be best if you stayed longer, after this is all over. I can teach you."

Evie gave my arm a light squeeze. "We'll save you a seat," she said with a wink, as she and Lily turned and melted back towards the crowd.

Wolfe stepped closer to me, drawing my attention back to him. A lone hand reached out, twirling a lock of my blonde hair between his fingers, eyes lazily looking me up and down before focusing back on my face.

"I'd really love to spend more time together, Rowan. You look positively ravishing tonight." I didn't miss the double meaning of his tone. He wanted much more than to spend time with me. I took a few steps back, my hair slipping from between his fingers as I met his grey eyes.

"I'm sure you would like to do a lot of things with me, Wolfe." Something about the night made me feel sassier than usual and more confident. "From what I hear, you do a lot of things with a lot of women."

A bark of laughter ripped out of him in surprise. "The gossip train has arrived at your station, I presume?"

I lifted my shoulder slightly in a shrug. "I appreciate your offer, but I would prefer to keep this relationship strictly professional. I try not to shit where I eat."

His eyes sparkled with humor, my comments not phasing him at all. He was persistent, stepping closer to me again and lowering his voice so only I could hear. "I'll respect your wishes if you promise to save me a dance."

"A dance?"

"Well, this is a party after all. We will eat, and then we will dance. Once the Mating Moon fully rises, things tend to get a little intense, and I'd prefer to keep you where I can keep my eye on you."

I tilted my head slightly to the left as I regarded him. I thought he was being flirty, and he was, but more than that, he was watching out for me. "Why is that?"

"There is a reason it's called the Mating Moon. It awakens some of our baser instincts as animals—the urge to mate. Mated pairs won't be able to resist and will pair off quickly, but unmated shifters will feel it too. You should prepare yourself; the moon will maximize your desire. If it gets to be too much, you should go home."

I scoffed. "I'll be fine. I'm not some sex-crazed teenager who can't control herself."

"It's not you I'm worried about." Wolfe smiled, and for a brief moment, I wondered if I had bitten off more than I could chew.

I PLOPPED DOWN IN THE SEAT EVIE HAD SAVED FOR ME, my mouth already watering at the feast in front of me. We sat on the edge of a long mahogany table that seemed to stretch endlessly, conversation and laughter blasting from all directions.

"This looks so freaking good." My mouth watered as I looked at the beautiful prime rib roast adorning the table, glistening with herbs and juices. I wasted no time reaching forward to carve myself a large slice, excitement erupting from me when I saw the big carafe labeled 'Au Jus' next to it.

"I love mating parties," Evie giggled as she watched me try to shovel the steak into my mouth without smearing my lipstick.

"Have you been to a lot of these?" I asked her between mouthfuls.

"This is my second. I can't wait until I'm eighteen and I can actually stay for the party. I need to get some." Her eyes sparkled at the prospect.

My mouth dropped open before I snapped it shut, remembering I still had food in my mouth. "Evie!"

"Shifters have needs! You're new, so you haven't felt it yet, but the Mating Moon has a very strong pull. Most unmated shifters hook up with each other during this time."

"I am not hooking up with anyone tonight. I can control myself." I laughed at the thought. I felt perfectly fine. A little flush from the lights and the side looks I was receiving, but I was fine.

Evie patted my leg gently before taking a bite of the pile of mashed potatoes she had scooped onto her plate. "Of course you can. It's not like it's a magic love potion that takes away your free will; it's just a strong suggestion."

We settled into a comfortable silence as we ate, and I watched as people of all backgrounds chatted and ate.

"I'm glad I came here," I said finally, giving her a small smile. The more I learned about this place and its people, the more I liked all of it. It gave a place to call home to many that wouldn't normally fit in elsewhere.

"Me too." She returned my smile before settling back in to finish her plate.

It wasn't much longer before a loud clanging bell sounded, and everyone rose from the tables in unison.

"What's happening?" I queried, standing along with everyone else. Evie grinned at me.

"It's party time. And my queue to leave. I'll see you tomorrow?" I nodded, and she gave me a tight hug before darting off toward the cabins along with a few others around her same age. Left alone, I looked around, quickly spotting Lily in the crowd and making a beeline for her.

"Rowan!" Her eyes lit up when she saw me, and it was immediately apparent she had already had a few to drink. I looked at the two glasses of wine she held, eyebrows high.

Her eyes rolled, an exasperated look on her face as she handed me a glass. "This one is for you, silly."

"Thanks." I chugged it down, trying to calm the nerves erupting in my belly as I looked around, taking stock of who had stayed behind. A lot of unfamiliar faces milled about as the moon started to rise, chatting and mingling with each other. A few heated glances turned my way, and the pit in my stomach grew as I felt my body start to flush with heat.

"See anybody you like?" Lily whispered to me conspiratorially, following my gaze.

"I'm not sleeping with anyone," I told her gruffly. "If anything,

I'm swearing off men for the rest of my life. They all suck," I said the last part loudly, hoping to scare away any potential suitors. My thoughts slipped back to Chad, and I cringed, regretting I'd ever let that man into my life.

"Fine, be sour all you want and waste that beautiful dress on your pity party." She twirled in a circle, her beauty radiating out from her. "I, on the other hand, am going to get laid." With a wink, she was gone, darting into the crowd to find her next victim.

All alone, I looked towards the direction of my cabin, contemplating skipping this altogether, when a lone figure caught my eye, hovering towards the edge of the gates. Squinting, I gasped when I realized, setting off in a beeline toward them as hip-hop music erupted behind me to a wave of loud cheers.

Drawing closer, I took in the tall drink of water that was Callan. He was not dressed for the occasion, wearing a simple pair of grey sweatpants and a solid black sweater despite the warm night. It didn't matter what he wore; he'd look good in everything. He leaned against the fence, hands in his pockets as he watched my approach. I didn't miss the way his eyes lingered on my body, and it sent a blistering scorch of heat through me.

"What are you doing here?" I asked as I came to a stop in front of him. He didn't strike me as the partying type. If I had to guess, he wasn't even invited, yet here he stood.

"I wanted to give you something," he said after a pause, still not moving.

"From all the way over here?"

He smirked slightly before pulling a long thin box from his pocket. I took it from him, ignoring the spark I felt when our fingers brushed slightly as I did. Hesitantly, I tugged the lid off, eyes widening when I saw what was inside.

Tears sprung to my eyes as I pulled out the thin knife from a hidden sheathe inside the box, the hilt a flattened black design of a skull that I'd recognize anywhere. This was made from the shift knob that used to be on SB.

"Thank you," I said softly, the shock at the kindness of the gift still coursing through me. "You have no idea how much this means to me."

He cleared his throat awkwardly, and I could have sworn I saw a slight flush creeping up his cheeks. "It's nothing. I figured you might need a weapon, considering your animal is next to useless if someone tries to attack you."

"Hey! I'm fierce!" I stomped on the ground, trying to drive my point home. How dare he insult my spirit animal.

"Yes, Rowan. You are fierce. Wildy, intimidatingly fierce. But your rabbit is not. She might be able to rob a carrot store, but she will not be able to fight a predator. My panther would eat her alive."

"Well, maybe you should," I blurted out before snapping my mouth shut. Did I really just say that? Oh my god.

Callan's gaze darkened, his mouth opening to reply until a cheery voice sounded from a few feet behind us.

"Fancy meeting you here," Wolfe said, and I whirled around to face him, sliding the knife back into its sheath and hiding it behind my back. I felt strong fingers slyly slide it from my hand, and I was grateful not to have to explain the present to Wolfe. We weren't doing anything wrong, but it felt like a moment I wanted to keep private.

"I was just coming to solidify our plans. For the witch's tracking spell."

Wolfe stared at him intensely. "Are you sure that's all that you came for? An interesting night you chose to stop by."

"I've been told I have impeccable timing," Callan replied, his gaze hot as he stared back.

Wolfe ripped his gaze from Callan's, turning back to me with a charming smile. "Rowan, it's time for that dance you promised me. The moon will rise soon."

"I'll see you in a few days?" I turned to look at Callan, who hadn't taken his eyes off Wolfe, the muscle in his jaw twitching. He nodded.

"Let's go then," I told Wolfe, walking off towards the party, back towards the blaring music and laughter. All this testosterone was making my skin itch, and for the first time that night, I was looking forward to letting loose and dancing the night away.

Chapter Eighteen

Wolfe led me to the dance floor just as the moon rose to the highest point in the sky, a slow song playing as couples swayed back and forth. I had been feeling flush before, but that was nothing compared to the wave of heat I felt as the luminescent glow settled on my skin. Warmth flowed through me, settling into a coiled lava pit at the base of my stomach as my entire body heated.

"Oh," I said breathlessly, and judging by the looks of the shifters around me, they were feeling it too. I noticed some newly-mated couples trying to get so close they could meld into one person.

"I told you," Wolfe said as he slid his large hands around my waist, pulling me closer. He dipped his head down, inhaling my scent with a deep breath. "You smell fucking amazing."

"Settle down." I threw my head back and laughed loudly. I was feeling good, but I still had self-control. He grinned at me, his pearly whites flashing.

"My charm doesn't work on you, does it?"

"Nope, sorry," I threw a light punch to his bicep, as friendly as I possibly could.

"Don't be sorry, love. I can respect that." He pulled me closer in a hug, and I ignored the spark of desire that it caused in me. That was the Mating Moon talking. My brain was still firmly intact and not focused on the bear shifter. Pulling away, he placed a gentle kiss on my forehead before he let me go completely. "If you'll excuse me, I will go grab us some drinks."

As he left, I stepped to the side of the dance floor, not wanting to look awkward standing alone. I should have been cold in the chilly night air, but the heat of my arousal kept me warm, as weird as that was. Little by little, it increased, fanning the slow burn in the pit of my stomach into a steady flame.

I waited a few minutes, observing the partygoers with amusement as the song changed, much more upbeat this time. My eyes landed on Lily, gyrating with a lion shifter I had met earlier on the dance floor. If they got any closer, he might be inside her, but I'm sure that is where he'd end up later if they kept it up. They weren't the only couple either; the dance floor was littered with pairs dancing suggestively with each other. Most of the mated couples seemed to have disappeared, no doubt to find somewhere more private to carry out their night.

Growing impatient, I looked around towards the outdoor bar they had set up for the night, wondering what was taking Wolfe so long. I spotted him standing a little too close to a pretty brunette by the dinner table, chatting with flirty expressions on their faces. I laughed to myself. It seemed I'd already been forgotten. Men.

"Water, please," I told the bartender as I strode up to the bar, taking matters into my own hands. I thought about getting a shot but cautioned against it. I wanted to be in full control tonight.

"Coming right up, gorgeous." His nostrils flared as he winked at me, and I immediately knew he was one of us. He set a cool water bottle down in front of me, the condensation wetting my hand.

"Thank you." I smiled, taking the cap off and chugging half the bottle. I'd thought the moon peak had been the worst of it, but I was feeling increasingly hot and bothered as the night wore on, and the heated looks from everyone were not helping anything.

"Rough night?" he asked as he wiped down the bar, keeping it clean.

"I've had rougher."

"Are you with the Clover pack? I've never seen you around here before. I'm on loan for the night from the Allentown pack."

"I'm new here. Rowan, nice to meet you." I reached an outstretched hand to shake, and he met it with a firm grasp, his skin hot. I felt my nether regions pulse at his touch, hungry for anything to fill the void, but I ignored it.

"Johnny, likewise," he smiled, his green eyes checking me out. I didn't know this man, but my body reacted anyway, my breathing speeding up. "You're not mated."

"No, I'm not." It wasn't a question, but I answered it anyway.

"I could come over to your place after this. I don't think I've seen someone as beautiful as you before. Maybe you're my mate." A stupidly goofy grin spread across his face, his eyes glazing slightly over.

I frowned at him. My body screamed at me to say yes, take him back to my bed, and have my dirty way with him, but I shook my head no.

Before he could respond, another man approached on my left. "I'll take two of whatever she's having. One for me, one for her."

"It's just water," I told the slender man who had approached, barely looking up at him.

"Well, knock it back." He pushed my bottle towards me, and I glared at him.

"Back up, buddy, I'm not interested."

"You can't blame him with an ass like that." Another voice, smooth like honey, on my right. I turned to look, seeing a gargantuan man next to me, his hot gaze scorching into mine.

"Excuse me?" I choked out.

"Out of all the unmated here, you smell the best. I think you could be my mate," the bear of a man whispered to me, his breath hot on my cheek as he bent closer to me.

"She's my mate," The slender man said confidently, sliding a hand around my waist and pulling me flush against him, my breasts pressed into his chest as I gasped in shock. "She smells like heaven. There's no way she could belong to anyone else."

I willed my traitorous limbs to push him away, out of my space, but I struggled, weak against his firm grasp. I was saved from having to scream for help when I felt the cold kiss of the familiar power that was Callan.

"She's not any of your mates," he growled low in his throat before he reached out, grabbing the slender man's wrist and bending it at an odd angle. The scream of pain told me he'd broken it, but I didn't care, a sense of relief cutting through the fiery haze roaring through me.

Callan gripped my arm, bending down and tossing me over one shoulder as if I was as light as a feather, walking off towards where the cabins stood.

"Put me down, asshole!" I ground out, the inferno inside me mixing with anger at being manhandled like a piece of meat.

"If I leave you here, a fight is going to break out," he said, continuing to walk to his destination. I looked around for help, and my fury only increased. Lily grinned from where she stood with her date, giving me a little wave when I caught her eye. Wolfe stood off to the side with his new boo, a knowing smirk on his face. When I saw them again, they were going to get an earful.

I wriggled from side to side, trying to make him put me down. Being this close to him, all I could think of was the heat of him underneath me as my body responded with a flood of arousal. My wiggling only succeeded in making me more uncomfortable as he lifted a hand and planted it firmly on my butt, holding me in place so I couldn't move. The fire exploded into life, consuming the last of any shame I had, and I couldn't help the slight moan that escaped me at his touch.

"Stop it." His voice was husky as he moved with purpose, now clearly heading towards my cabin on the edge of the tree line.

"Stop what?" I said breathily as I tried to wiggle again, this time for a different purpose. I hypothesized if I wiggled in just the right way, I might be able to give myself some relief. A scientist I was not, but I sure knew how to wet my own whistle.

His grip tightened on my ass, and I moaned again. "I'm taking you to your cabin, where you will take a very cold shower and stay inside."

"Or," I replied sweetly, "You could come inside with me."

Tomorrow I'd probably be embarrassed, but with the moon in full effect, I didn't care. I wanted someone, and Callan was at the top of my list.

"I will not sleep with you." The flatness of his tone was not lost on me as he reached the door to my cabin, awkwardly opening the door with one hand as the other one still gripped my cheeks. "My time for that has gone."

He plopped me down on the sofa, shutting the cabin door behind him. He turned to look at the door, muttering a curse under his breath.

"Do you not have a damn lock on this damn thing?" The edges of his words were tinged with accent, his Scottish lilt coming out with his frustration.

"I don't think I need one here." I pulled myself up on my knees on the couch, squirming under the weight of desire coursing through me. The conversation helped, but only a little.

"You do tonight. When I leave, those men will try to woo you."

"Woo me? Who even says woo anymore?" I retorted boldly. "Maybe I'll let them in and have some fun."

I wouldn't, but he didn't have to know that. No amount of horny would make me go back out there while I had him here.

He growled low in his chest, animalistic. "You will do no such thing. Go cool off and sleep; I'll stand guard."

"I will. After you leave, I can take care of myself." In more ways than one. I tried to inflect irritation into my tone but only succeeded in sounding like a phone sex operator in training.

"No, you can't." He held a hand up, halting the protest he knew was coming. He rounded on me, face coming so close I was tempted to reach out and taste him. "The Mating Moon is intense, but it's still manageable. Those men shouldn't be behaving that way."

"Then why?" I whispered; eyes focused on his lips. He snapped his fingers a few times to get my attention, and I dragged my eyes up to his with sheer willpower. I was running on fumes at this point, desperately horny fumes.

"You, Rowan. Whatever it is that makes you special. On this night? You smell fucking irresistible."

"You seem to be resisting just fine." My hand dipped toward the pooling wetness between my thighs, aching for relief.

His gaze darkened, and he backed away suddenly like he had been burned. My resolve wavered as I fought the urge to reach out to him, pull him back into me and have my way with him.

"I can control myself."

"Can you?" It was a dare, and we both knew it. I should have tried to control myself, but under the spell of the moon, I didn't want to. I knew exactly what I wanted.

He observed me then, squirming on the couch, wheels turning in his head as he figured out how to deal with me. He charged forward, gripping my arm and throwing me back over his shoulder. I gasped in surprise, warmth pooling in my center, thinking he would have his way with me.

Marching into the bathroom, he shoved back the curtain, turning the spray on full blast to the coldest setting. Shifting my weight to the front of his arms, he gently set me down in the frigid water, fully clothed. I shrieked at the initial shock of it, steam forming around me even in the blast of the cold downpour. It took a few moments for my body to acclimate, the cascading water feeling like a gentle caress all over my body. Callan watched me for a long minute before he turned on his heel, marching out of the room with a slam of the door.

Frustrated, I worked my way out of the dress, hoping that it would be salvageable tomorrow. I leaned against the back of the shower wall, letting the water cascade over my now-naked body. The blaze inside me raged on, begging me to satiate it. I looked to the door where Callan had left, thoughts of him racing through my mind.

Stretching my left hand downwards, I found my center immediately. My fingers circled my clit like a mad woman, the first orgasm washing over me in no time, leaving me gasping for breath. My limbs trembled, the liquid heat inside of me boiling over. My teeth clenched as I slipped one finger, then a second, inside of me, pumping along in rhythm with the strokes on my clit.

I moaned loudly, memories of my dream with Callan flooding my head and fueling the fire. I'm sure he could hear me, but I was too far gone to care.

I would have done anything to have him in the shower with me, fingers buried deep. I cried out at the thought, my hand working faster between my thighs.

My other hand reached up and tugged a nipple, softly at first but then harder, the pain stoking the climax I knew was fast approaching.

Come for me. His dreamy words echoed in my mind, catapulting me over the edge.

"Oh, fuck!" I screamed, wave after wave of pleasure rushing through me, black spots dancing across my vision. I rode it out, letting my fingers slip out of myself as the water coursed over me.

Panting heavily, I sobbed softly when I realized it had done nothing to assuage my hunger. If anything, the flames had been stoked even higher, my body a bundle of barely contained heat. I slammed my head backward against the shower, letting out a growl of frustration at my predicament. I'd never been this worked up in my life. What the hell was going on?

I raised a weak hand and turned off the shower, pulling myself up and out on shaky legs, wrapping a towel around myself. I clenched my thighs together as I continued to pulse with need. Opening the door to the bathroom, my eyes adjusted to see Callan sitting in the armchair across the living room, facing me. In the semi-darkness, I couldn't make out his expression.

"Callan?" My voice was low, laced with desire.

"Go to bed now, Rowan." His voice was thick, filled with something I couldn't understand in my hazy state.

"I can't." It came out as more of a whine than I meant it to, but it was true all the same. I gasped as a lance of lust ripped through me. "It's getting worse."

He muttered a curse under his breath, fists clenching on his thighs. "I can't, Rowan. Not like this."

"Please," I moaned, falling to my knees as another pang went through me.

"You don't know what you're asking," he told me, not moving from where he sat. "The moon is-"

"I'm an adult," I told him, my breath quickening as I stared him down. I could feel the effects of the moon, but part of this was just me. My attraction to Callan that I'd been fighting since I got here. "And I want this. I can't make it through the night like this."

He stood up and paced back and forth for a moment before he turned to look at me. "I will help you, but this is a one-time thing. We cannot do this again."

"I get it." And I did. He had already found his mate; he didn't want me. This would be the only night with him I would get. "Now shut up and help me."

Callan rushed over to me, pulling me into his arms as he headed into the bedroom. He tossed me onto the bed, and I whimpered in anticipation. His gaze burned into me, and it was then I realized my towel must have fallen off at some point, and now I was completely baring myself to him. I should have felt self-conscious but didn't, as I spread my legs wide in invitation.

"I'm not fucking you. That's for your mate to do," Callan replied, a sour edge to his tone. "But I can still take care of you."

He leaned over me, meeting my eyes until I whined, my hips gyrating toward him. A dark chuckle escaped him, his earthy scent washing over me, assaulting my senses. I moaned, not even the slightest bit embarrassed that he hadn't touched me yet.

He didn't make me wait, knowing I needed this now, and dove straight in. The touch of his tongue on my pussy had me screaming, my hands twisting into the sheet below me as I writhed in pleasure against his relentless attack. He sucked my clit, circling it expertly with his tongue. Whereas some guys like to spell out the alphabet, this guy was writing a whole damn novel. I rocketed through my third orgasm of the night, the pleasure stronger than anything I'd ever felt.

"It's working," I managed to gasp out between moans, the fire inside me lessening only slightly, like dousing one tree in a miles-long forest fire.

I expected Callan to relent a little, but he didn't, instead reaching his hand down and slipping two fingers into my tight hole. His fingers were much thicker than mine, and it took me a few seconds to adjust to the new size, walls squeezing tightly around his fingers. He glanced up at me, emerald eyes flecked with gold, blazing brighter than I'd ever seen them. My breath caught in my throat, entranced, before he broke eye contact. Returning to his mission, his tongue stroked away at my every nerve ending, building me right back up.

"Oh, my god," I cried out, chest still heaving from the last one. I reached down and threaded my fingers through his hair, bunching the coarse strands in my grip as I writhed in pleasure.

His free hand began to wander, rubbing over my thighs before sliding higher, stopping only when he reached my breasts. He rolled a nipple between his fingers and simultaneously slammed his fingers into me hard, fingers finding that special spot inside me, sending me into oblivion as another wave of ecstasy crashed over me.

"Callan!" I cried out as I came, and I felt a breathy chuckle against me as he languidly lapped at my sensitive folds, riding it out. Sensing I needed a break, he paused and lifted his head, eyes hooded. The fire had faded more, but not enough, and the sight of my juices glistening on his perfect lips had me squirming with need. Again.

"Better?" he asked thickly. I knew he didn't want to be with me, but a part of me hoped he was as into this as I was.

"It's getting there, but-" I gasped as another surge hit me, begging him to continue his magic. My hips lifted of their own accord, arching towards his mouth.

"How long is this supposed to last?" I cried out as his fingers returned to their relentless task.

"No rush," he said softly before diving back into it fully, his tongue teasing my clit in slow torturous circles. I had no time to dwell on that comment as the familiar pressure of release built again, a roller coaster that I couldn't get off.

I wasn't sure I even wanted to.

Chapter Nineteen

I stood on the edge of the same cliff from before, the wind roaring through the air as it whirled around me. In front of me stood the hooded figure, unwavering against the onslaught of the wind.

"Who are you?" I tried to shout, but the words were torn from my throat and whipped away before I could make a sound.

The figure rushed forward faster than it should be possible, and I took a step back in response. My eyes opened wide as I felt the cliff's edge, throwing my arms out in a windmill gesture to try to steady myself before falling to my death.

I screamed as I lost my footing and tumbled backward, my eyes clenched shut as I braced for impact. Slim fingers wrapped around my wrist firmly, and my fall halted as I was yanked back onto solid ground.

I opened my eyes and gasped as I came face to face with the cloaked figure. Familiar brown eyes met mine as I looked into a mirror image of myself. She smiled at me before leaning in to put her lips next to my ear.

"They're coming," she said in my voice so softly I barely heard her. I pulled my head back and stared at her in confusion. Before I could respond and ask her what the hell she meant by that, she pressed both hands to my chest and pushed me off the cliff.

Sunlight streamed through the windows as I woke with a start, hitting me right in the eyes. I shook off the strange dream, chalking it up to the remnants of the Mating Moon. I stretched lazily, relishing it as my back cracked with the movement, feeling more relaxed than I had in a long time. A jolt of disappointment ran through me as I realized I was alone, but I shouldn't have been surprised.

The memories of the night before swam through my mind, and I felt my cheeks flush in embarrassment and arousal. I couldn't believe I threw myself at him like that. It had been an amazing night; he had brought me to orgasm so many times I couldn't count before the moon's spell had faded enough to let me fall asleep. I'm not even sure when Callan had left, as satiated and exhausted as I had been. I was thankful I wouldn't have to see him for a few days. The witch's spell wouldn't be ready for a few more days.

As much as I tried, he hadn't let me touch him once, and it bothered me. Not because he didn't let me, he made it very clear that nothing further would happen. No, what bothered me was how much I wanted to, even now, without the haze of the moon influencing my decisions. To touch him, reciprocate the pleasure he had given me, take him to my bed, and make him mine. Oh, boy. I've lost my damn mind.

I heaved a frustrated breath, pulling myself out of bed and stumbling to the bathroom to do my morning routine. I didn't have anything on the roster today, but I figured I could see Lily. I'm sure she was dying to know how my night went, and I certainly wanted to check on hers. The last time I saw her, she was attempting to demonstrate how to climb a man like a tree. Finishing up, I ran a quick brush through my blonde locks, throwing on a basic outfit of ripped blue jeans and a loose-fitting white T-shirt, throwing my signature leather jacket over it.

I stepped out into the living room, everything looking exactly as I had left it, except for a long box on the couch that I recognized. Stepping closer, I picked it up gently, a small smile stretching at the corners of my lips as I opened the box. The knife Callan gave me lay in the box, and I was struck once again by the thoughtfulness of the gift. I had thought SB was completely totaled, beyond salvage, but knowing I still had a piece of her with me made me whole again. Grieving a car may seem stupid, but she'd been a better constant in my life than any person ever had.

I lifted the knife out of the box, surprised to find a simple leather sheath lying underneath it along with a belt, the perfect size to clip around my jeans or thigh if I tightened it enough. Callan was nothing if not prepared. Given what I was wearing, I looped the buckle around my jeans, sliding the knife into place. It was heavier than I was used to, but it was a comforting weight to have.

I slid my phone into my back pocket, heading towards the front door to find Lily. Judging by the light outside, it was still pretty early, the afternoon sun not yet out to play. I stopped in my tracks when I realized there was a note taped to the inside of my door.

Witch's timeline moved up. Two Days. Be ready. -C

He really had a way with words. Another reminder that last night had meant nothing to him. Move on, Rowan.

I yanked my front door open with a little more force than necessary, charging out into the crisp fall morning. The chatter of the birds chirping as they flitted through the trees helped to calm my frayed nerves, and by the time I'd reached Lily's cabin, I'd almost put last night behind me. Almost.

I knocked on her pale green door, admiring the personal touches she'd put into her home. She'd weaved plant life between the log panels, threading intricate patterns of earthy vines.

Colorful lights were strung up around the door. There was no mistaking this house for Lily's, not in a million years.

"Hey." The door opened with a rush, and my friend stood on the other side. I gasped in shock as my eyes met her second pair, staring straight at me from their enviously perky perch on her chest.

"Lily!" I exclaimed, holding my hand out in front of my eyes to block my view. "Put some clothes on!"

"You really need to get over that." She closed the door briefly, and I heard her shuffle around before she opened it again, now wearing a short cotton crop top that stopped right over her belly button. I was thankful to see she at least had underwear on.

"You alone?" I asked her as I stepped inside. It was my first time in her place, and I stopped to admire the room. The inside was just as eccentric as the outside. The living room was painted a pastel pink, with stars and flowers scattered in waves throughout the house. Instead of my cabin's plain dull lighting, she had a bright chandelier that hung from the ceiling. It should have looked out of place with its sparkly exterior, but it was just another layer to the madness in this room.

"Yeah, Diego left at dawn. He never stays long," she said it so casually. It was clear it wasn't her first rodeo with this Diego guy.

"Is he your boyfriend or something?" I knew the answer before she even started laughing.

"No, silly. He's just an occasional visitor." The lusty wink she gave me had me giggling.

"And how many visitors like these guys do you have?"

"As many as I want," she said loftily, and I'd never admired her more than I did then.

"And how about you? You had all the boys hot and bothered last night, unusually so. Even Wolfe looked like he was having an issue."

"I don't know what that was. Everyone says I smell different." I couldn't help the exasperation that edged into my tone. "I'm hoping the witch can help me figure it out."

"Oliver?" she asked. At my nod, she said, "If anyone can, it's him. Rumor is he only surfaced on the witch scene a few years ago, but he's more powerful than their own High Priestess. He chooses not to take power."

No wonder he'd been able to freeze Callan so easily. If all witches could do a fraction of what Oliver had done, the shifters would stand no chance in a head-to-head battle. "I'll ask him."

"Enough of the boring talk. Tell me what I really want to know." Her stare bored into the side of my head as I pretended not to hear her and instead looked around the room. The silence stretched too long, and I fought the smile that tugged at my lips.

"Rowan!" she barked at me, and the smile turned into a full-blown grin as she exploded. "You do not get to be a fireman carried by one of the hottest men alive to your bedroom and not tell me the details!"

"Nothing happened," I tried to lie, my heartbeat speeding up, and her eyes narrowed at me, head cocked to one side. I didn't want her to know what had happened between us. It would only give her false expectations for something I knew would never happen.

"Stop lying," she said. "Tell me, just how big is it?"

"I have no idea," I told her, doing my best to look sad and pitiful. It wasn't hard. "We didn't have sex."

Technically, not a lie.

She was speechless for a moment as she floundered for words. "You didn't throw him down and jump his bones?"

"I tried. He wouldn't go for it." I shrugged, the sour look on my face entirely genuine. "He said he's done with all that."

"Sex?" she screeched, incredulous. "I don't see how anyone can live without sex—especially not a shifter. We're like a bunch of over-sexed bunnies. Oh, sorry." She cut an apologetic look at my sharp one.

"He's already had his mate. You said it before, only one mate per person."

"It's pretty remarkable that he didn't lose his mind," Lily commented, pulling a few containers of yogurt from her fridge.

"I'm sure he has lost his mind," I muttered as I caught the yogurt, popping it open with one hand as I accepted the spoon she offered.

"Seriously. Most mates who lose their other half die quickly. It's very rare for them to be okay without them."

I spooned a few mouthfuls of yogurt, delighting in the tang of strawberry as it hit my tongue. "What would make the difference? Why would he stay intact longer?"

"Mental fortitude, I guess. Maybe his Alpha powers. He was a very strong Alpha in his prime. Many wanted him to take over for the Supreme one day. He was just and fair, and that's hard to come by sometimes."

"How do you know so much about it?"

"Wolfe," Lily said wistfully, lost in memory. They both seemed to have moved on, but it was clear there was still a lot of love there. Lily shook her head, dragging herself back to the present. "He's been different since you got here."

"Wolfe?" I scoffed. "I have no interest in being a notch on his belt."

"Callan," she said firmly. My face scrunched in disbelief; she must have been losing her mind too. "He has never come to a Mating party in all the years I've been here."

"He was just bringing me something," I gestured to the knife strapped to my belt. "Something to protect myself."

Lily rolled her eyes. "Rowan, don't be stupid. He could have given that to you at any time. Nothing would be able to harm you in this compound. He came here to ensure nobody tried to steal you away to their evil sex dungeons."

I threw my now empty yogurt container, satisfied when it bonked her on the head, little specks of pink yogurt dotting her hair. "Stop it. He told me himself. He had his mate, and she died, and that's it for him."

She opened her mouth to argue, but I gave her a sharp look,

willing this conversation to end. All this talk about Callan had soured my good mood, and I would do whatever I had to do to change the subject. She cleared her throat awkwardly.

"What's the plan for today? Any witch visits?"

"Nope, not for a few days. I'm all yours today." She lit up with that, nearly bouncing in her seat with excitement.

"That's the best news I've had all week! Let's get Evie. We can go into town and catch a movie, grab some lunch. Have an all-out girls' day?"

I grinned back at her. A day of fun and relaxation as far away from my panther problems sounded like a great time. "Let me just get dressed, and I'll meet you outside."

Lily was out in record time, wearing a similar outfit to mine of jeans and a form-fitting black blouse that hugged her in all the right spots. Even when she tried to look casual, she was effortless. We shuffled toward the back of the compound I recalled from my tour, where Evie lived in a smaller version of our cabins specifically designed for more transient shifters and guests.

We walked through the rows of houses. Most of them looked to be vacant. "Why doesn't Evie live in a cabin like I do?" I questioned.

"Those cabins are usually only for permanent members. You were an exception to the rule. I think Wolfe wanted to keep you where he could see you, honestly." It made sense now why I'd been assigned the cabin directly in front of his house.

"She's not a permanent member?" That seemed ridiculous to me, given how integrated she was with the pack.

"You can't join a pack officially until you turn eighteen, unless you were born into it." She leaned closer to me in a conspiratorial whisper. "When her birthday comes around, I'm going to ask her if she'll officially become my roommate."

My heart filled with joy at her sentiment. It seemed like Evie had been through a lot, and a permanent home with someone as fun as Lily sounded like the right move for her. "I can't wait to see that."

She bumped my shoulder happily as we approached the street Evie lived. As we turned a corner, a familiar scent of earth and Jasmine taunted my nose, dancing just out of range. I halted in my tracks, my head tilted up in the air as I tried to focus my nose.

"What's wrong?" Lily asked, concern written across her face as she tried to scent what I was and couldn't.

"They're here." Was all I said before I took off, my instincts and my nose leading further down the street. I paused briefly before I zeroed in on a small house near the end of the block. Lily's footfalls pounded behind me as I raced on, blind to everything but the scent I chased.

The scent led me straight to the white paneled door, and I took a shaky breath as I stretched out a hand, pushing the already open door wider. My other hand flew to my buckle, unlatching and withdrawing the knife, holding it in front of me in a protective gesture. As the door opened wider, I was hit with a strong scent of copper, and I sneezed against the assault.

Stepping inside, I took a second to take in my surroundings and regretted it immediately. The walls of the room were splattered with crimson, the copper stench of blood filling my nostrils. My heart seized as I took in the lone figure splayed out on the bed. Still in her dress from last night, Evie was splayed out on the bed, on full display. She would have looked like she was sleeping peacefully if not for the gaping hole in the center of her chest where her heart should have been.

I ran right back out, barely making it before throwing up my meager yogurt breakfast all over the gravel beneath me, tears streaming down my face.

"Don't go in there!" I managed to scream to Lily, but I was already too late. Her agonized roar ripped through the quiet morning, a sound I knew I'd hear in my nightmares for years to come.

Chapter Twenty

"We need to act now!" Lily growled, fury and anguish lacing her tone as she slammed her fists on the table.

Nearly the entire pack was crammed into the cafeteria, which had been repurposed into a makeshift assembly hall. The room that had once been alive with the sound of outraged cries and muffled sobs silenced immediately with Lily's outburst. She was a submissive wolf, but I shivered as a small burst of power rippled through the room.

"Mark my words," Wolfe's presence commanded attention from where he stood at the head of the room. "We will find the monster who did this. And they will pay."

"Then why are we still here?" Lily challenged. I looked between them, hoping she didn't accidentally challenge the Alpha.

Wolfe had been the first person we called as soon as we saw what happened to Evie, and he'd wasted no time calling an emergency pack meeting. I wrapped my arms around myself in a comforting gesture, remembering the horror I had witnessed. All the blood, the fear she must have felt as she died all alone. A small sob escaped me before I swallowed it down.

I'd have all the time in the world to mourn Evie after this bastard was dead.

"I need to make sure the rest of my pack stays safe. No one should have been able to penetrate our wards." His red-rimmed eyes looked around the room, making eye contact with everyone he could. I looked down before he could get to me. I'd been the one tasked with finding this killer, Evie's killer, and all I'd done so far was give my blood to an all-powerful witch. What if I had been the cause of this?

The guilt wormed in, burrowing a permanent place in my heart.

"Witches are on their way to check the wards," Wolfe carried on, his fiery alpha power draping over us like a blanket, my skin tingling under its weight. "Even so, no one goes anywhere without a buddy from now on. Anyone who lives in a private cabin, move."

A few angry shouts sounded but were cut off as I felt the heat of his power increase around us until all fell silent. The charming playboy was completely gone now, and in his place stood a fearsome leader, out for blood. "We will work in shifts to patrol until the culprit is brought to justice. In pairs, two-hour shifts at a time. See Malachi after this meeting for the schedule. If you have questions, take it up with him. Rowan and Lily, see me after. Everyone else is dismissed."

The grumbling mass of people slowly exited the cafeteria, heading towards Malachi, who stood outside with their assignments. I took a moment to admire Wolfe and his pack. Even in a devastating situation like this one, he confidently led his people. Many of them gave him a nod or a pat on the shoulder on their way out, their trust and respect for him obvious. I wondered if this was how Callan's pack had reacted to him before everything happened.

A few minutes later, the room stood empty, only the three of us left standing. The heavy air settled between us as the reality of our situation sank in further.

"Have you spoken to Callan?" Wolfe directed towards me, eyes serious.

I frowned, trying to push through the hazy shock that still plagued me. My hand flew to my back pocket, remembering the cell phone I'd stuffed there this morning. I pulled it out, swiping across the screen and unlocking it with a faint whooshing noise as it opened for me. "I completely forgot. I'll call him now."

I stepped over to the side where I'd have a little more privacy, ignoring the low murmurs of their voices as I searched the phone. It didn't take me long to find Callan's number, given I only had four numbers. Evie's name blinked up at me from under his, my heart wrenched in my chest. I'd never even gotten to use it. I pushed the green call icon, the ringtone almost comforting in my ear as it trilled.

"What?" I swallowed hard, my body heating in response to the low timbre of his voice despite the circumstances. His tone was as sour as usual, like last night had never happened. I shut my eyes, hoping that would be enough to keep out any unwanted feelings the previous night had drummed up, choosing to dwell in my sadness and anger instead.

"Rowan?" he repeated, pulling me from my thoughts.

"You need to get down here as soon as possible," I finally said, unable to keep the crack out of my voice. "Evie was...Evie was murdered last night."

Callan was silent so long I thought he might have hung up before I heard a string of curses in a language I didn't understand.

"I'll be there in ten," was all he said before the line went dead.

"How could they have gotten through the wards?" Callan demanded. The four of us sat gathered around a table, still in the cafeteria. Callan had made it in ten minutes, charging in like a bat out of hell, fury coming out of his pores. I wasn't sure if he'd looked at me, given I was doing my best not to look at him.

"Only a very powerful magic user could have done such a thing. Our wards are made by the High Priestess herself, making Clover Pack one of the most well-protected packs on the entire west coast. I made sure of it after...." Wolfe trailed off at Callan's glower. After his mate had slaughtered the whole pack and he killed her.

Unease trickled through me. How was I supposed to catch a powerful shifter with witches backing them? I was a brand-new shifter who turned into a bunny, and the most combat training I'd done was during my training with Lily this week. I might be able to take down a mugger, but a shapeshifting murderer with magic? I was way in over my head, and the urge to run was stronger than ever.

The panic seeped in for a split second before hitting my resolve. I was here for a reason. I'd learned more about myself in the last week than ever before. I had so many more questions, and this was the only place I could find it. And with my connection to the scent, I was the only person who could help them track this bastard down.

I hadn't forgotten about the ten thousand dollars Wolfe had promised me, but if I was honest with myself, I didn't care about that anymore. I'd only been here a short time, but these people had shown me so much acceptance, so much about myself, and I'd only begun to scratch the surface. Evie was my friend.

They'll be lucky if they find a body after I got my hands on this asshole.

"RO!" Lily barked at me, snapping me out of my thoughts.

"What? Sorry." I blinked stupidly, so lost in my head that I hadn't heard a word they were saying.

"Did you catch the same scent?"

"Yes. It was unmistakable."

"We need to see Oliver." Callan's face was a mask of determination and anger. "We can't wait any longer."

"Call the witch then," Lily commanded, pure ferocity in her eyes. Evie had been like a younger sister to her, and she wore her pain outward.

Callan shook his head slightly, meeting my gaze for the first time that day. "We need to take him by surprise."

"Why?" Wolfe demanded.

"It takes a powerful witch to interfere with a ward placed by a High Priestess. And Oliver is said to be more powerful than her. I don't think we can trust him."

"But why would he double-cross us like that?" I asked. "We paid him."

Wolfe snorted, answering before Callan could. "It makes sense. Witches only choose their own side. If our enemy offered more, it's entirely possible we were betrayed."

Heat simmered in my gut, begging to be unleashed upon my nearest enemy, but I tamped it down. Barely. I'd been stupid to think I could trust Oliver. Of course, I couldn't trust the all-powerful witch who wanted my blood as payment. Then a thought struck me. How could I have been so stupid?

"Could my blood have been what helped them get across?"

"Rowan, you should never give your blood to a witch," Lily admonished.

"I don't understand what the big deal is." I lifted one shoulder, trying to shrug it off. "It was just a little blood."

"Sometimes I forget you're so new to this," Wolfe huffed, before leveling me with a serious gaze. "Blood amplifies their spells, no matter what kind. A witch might be able to make a tree grow tall from a pile of dirt but give her an Alpha's blood, and she could create a whole damn forest."

"And your blood..." Lily trailed off, her sentence hanging unfinished in the air.

"We don't know what your blood can do," Wolfe said finally. As their words sunk in, I avoided looking at Lily, my eyes glancing off hers and firmly affixing to the table. It could be my fault that they could even get into the compound in the first place. I said nothing, the guilt hanging over me like a death sentence.

"We're wasting time," Callan said tersely, the slight taste of his accent rolling off his tongue. "Besides the similarities between victims and the missing hearts, we have nothing. Without this tracking spell, we'll lose our only potential lead."

"We're coming with you," Wolfe said firmly, no room for questioning in his tone. "This is personal now."

Lily nodded fervently. Callan opened his mouth, no doubt to object like the stubborn mule he was, but I shot a swift kick at his shin from where I sat across from him. A surprised yelp came out of him instead, and I tried not to relish the satisfaction that gave me. His emerald eyes glared at me, meeting my eyes for the first time today, but I held my ground, holding my gaze steady. After a long moment, he heaved a sigh of resignation, and I broke eye contact before it got too intense, satisfied he'd let them come along.

We needed all the help we could get.

Chapter Twenty-One

As we drove to Oliver's shop, I was glad for the extra company. With Lily tagging along, I had a great excuse to sit in the back seat, as far away from Callan as possible. With all the chaos, we'd had no time to be alone, and I was grateful for it, not wanting to deal with the painfully awkward scene that would be. Best case scenario, I avoid him for the rest of my life.

Night had fallen when we turned into the parking lot, the surrounding trees casting shadows along the ground like an otherworldly circus. Callan jerked to a stop directly in front of the shop, turning in his seat to pin us with his stare.

"Stay alert. He's not going to like this intrusion. Knife out, Rowan." He exited the car, and we all followed suit. I pulled the knife from its sheath that I'd strapped to my right leg, a comforting weight in my hand. I noticed no one else held a weapon in hand, but I did not doubt that all of them were much more deadly than I was, even in human form.

We walked through the front door, the shop still open as the day wound down to an end. Callan stormed in first, Wolfe and Lily close on his heels. I drew in behind them all, my knife held out awkwardly in front of me in what I hoped was a defensive position.

The store looked the same as before, organized chaos. Oliver stood behind the counter. His brown eyes narrowed on us, so dark they might have been black, as I felt the telltale charge of his magic start to build in the air.

Callan would not be caught off guard this time as he wrapped his power around him, the air cooling considerably as it leeched off of him. All three shifters sharpened their nails into menacing claws. Now I understood why they didn't carry weapons.

"Was it you?" Callan bit out, low and menacing.

"If you're asking if I'm the witch that broke your silly little wards, then no." He spoke plainly, his stare direct. All three of their ears perked, and by the set of their shoulders, they'd detected no sign of deception. But still, I wasn't convinced. "If I wanted to attack the shifters, I'd have done it long ago."

"How do we know you're not lying?" I threw out, eyes sparking with suspicion. He shrugged, grinning at us through cracked teeth. "That's not my problem. But as a show of good faith, I called in a favor the second I heard about the attack. Bought an extraordinarily expensive tracking spell on the black market. We will get much better results if we cast the spell while the memory is fresh. We can talk payment later."

Wolfe and Callan exchanged a look before they relaxed, magic dissipating. After a glance at Wolfe, Lily also withdrew her claws. I followed, stowing my knife back in its home. At his prompt, we followed Oliver behind his countertop and through the beaded drapes he had covering a large archway to the back room of the shop.

The room we were led to was much sparser than the clutter of the shop behind us. All of us fit inside comfortably, given that there was a giant symbol etched onto a raised moonstone platform in the center. It wasn't anything I recognized, as beautiful as it was, the stone a brilliant grey-blue shimmer. The carving was shaped like an S, with dozens of lines branching off, weaving into intricate twists and turns. A tall rustic cauldron stood in the center at waist height, steam bubbling from inside. A small table in one corner held what looked to be a map.

"How does this work?" I asked, awed at the new world I was now a part of.

"It's very simple. You will step on the dais with me and drink the potion. The map will help pinpoint the location with a scrying crystal." He nodded over to the corner and looking closer, I realized it was a complete map of the city and surrounding areas. He made it sound so simple.

We approached the dais, easily managing the steep incline needed to step up. Oliver clapped his hands, flames flicking to life in the groove between the platform and the ground, encasing us in a literal ring of fire. I took a step back in surprise, Oliver's hand darted out to grab mine and pull me forward before the flames could singe me.

"Should have warned you about that," he said with a conspiratorial wink. I could have sworn I heard a faint growl over the roar of the fire, but the flames completely obscured our vision. Beads of sweat trickled down my back as the heat pressed into me.

Taking a steadying breath, I righted myself and approached the cauldron. Steam rose from it as it bubbled and popped, a sickly orange color churning inside. I could see sprigs of herbs I couldn't identify, chunks of chopped-up materials I didn't recognize. I almost lost my lunch when I noticed a long, spindly feather poking out of the concoction.

"There's no way I'm drinking this."

"If you want any hope of catching this killer, then you must." The look he gave me was pitying as a small metal cup he hadn't had earlier materialized in his hand. He dipped it into the boiling concoction, pulling out a generous portion of the potion. "Don't you want revenge? For Ella, wasn't it?"

"Evie." I glowered at him, begrudgingly taking the offered cup

167

from his hand. I expected heat, but the cup was cool to the touch, and there was no longer any steam radiating from it as I had seen before.

Oliver leaned in so close I could smell the coffee he must have had recently, his head bowed low. "The fire is my own personal cone of silence. We can hear them, but they won't be able to hear us." I stared blankly at him.

"This is not the only potion I made," he said slyly, giving my waiting friends a glance from the side to make sure they couldn't see. The fire roared around us stronger than ever, masking us from sight. I was now completely sure I heard a growl that sounded suspiciously like Callan.

Oliver pulled out a small, thin vial from his pocket, only large enough to hold a few tablespoons of clear liquid. Looking closer, I noticed a sparkly substance floating throughout the tube, almost like specks of gold.

"I've been studying your blood, researching the spell that still entraps you. Drink this, and it will break."

I couldn't help the excited gasp that escaped me, but at the same time, an overwhelming feeling of dread came over me. "What kind of spell is it? What's wrong with me?"

An approving look swam into his eye as he looked at me. "I'm giving you the vial so you can choose, Rowan. The spell that binds you is powerful and was put on you for your safety. This is not a choice to make lightly."

"There is ancient magic on you. Magic most people don't understand. I can feel it radiating off you in waves, Rowan. I couldn't discern exactly what the spell is binding, barely enough to make this potion. You may not want to know what lies underneath; the journey will not be easy."

"Journey?" It was naïve to think it would be that easy, but dammit, I wanted something in life to be easy for once.

"To break this spell, you must die first. The spell is tied directly into your life force." Seeing my look of shock, he continued hurriedly, "This potion is designed to stop your heart for one minute and then restart it."

"And if it doesn't go well?"

"You'll just have to trust me."

Chapter Twenty-Two

I didn't want to break it, so I raised my hand, shoving the vial into my bra. Oliver raised his brows at the movement, which I returned with a withering glare. I was thankful he made it, but I had a lot to think about before taking it. If I ever decided to take it. "It's precious cargo."

A feminine shout reached above the roar of the flames, followed swiftly by a ferocious growl and a yelp of pain. Eyes wide, I focused on Oliver. "We should hurry up and do this now."

He nodded in agreement, pushing the potion up toward my mouth. "Bottoms up." I grimaced but obliged, reaching one hand up to pinch my nose closed as I did. It went down easy, chilled like I had just taken it out of the refrigerator. Swallowing the last gulp, I released my hold on my nose and almost gagged at the remnants of the flavor on my tongue. It was like a mix of stinky feet and dog pee, but I forced myself to hold it down, staring at the ceiling for a moment to find my strength.

"Now close your eyes and give me your hands." I closed my eyes and outstretched my hand toward him. He gripped them, his hands clammy with sweat, but I bit back the sassy remark I had ready.

He chanted low, in a language I couldn't understand, and as he did, I felt his hands warm to the touch. They got hotter and hotter, almost to a blistering temperature. I held on for as long as possible, and the chanting stopped just when I was about to hit a breaking point. With one final surge of blistering heat, he dropped my hands, and I was surprised to see they looked just as they always did, with no burns anywhere.

"Now we scry," he said softly, watching me closely. He seemed satisfied and nodded before raising his hands out in front of him, lowering them gently. The flames dissipated with his movements, revealing a scene I never thought I'd see.

Callan stood to one side, cuts and scrapes already healing in various spots all over his exposed skin. Lily stood protectively in front of the dais, still in human form, with her claws extended. Wolfe was on her other side, scratches littering his arms as well. Small droplets of blood dripped off her claws and onto the floor as she glared down at Callan, who, if I didn't know any better, appeared to be sulking.

"What the hell happened to you guys?" I asked as I jumped off the small platform, my boots thudding as they hit the ground. I looked from person to person, nostrils flaring as I could smell the anger wafting off them.

"Callan got impatient and wanted to jump into the fire to save you," Lily said irritably. "We stopped him."

"Save me?" I snorted. "I can save myself. Besides, it was perfectly safe."

"We couldn't hear you," Callan said defensively, not meeting my eyes. "Or see you. I don't trust this witch." He spat the last word like it was dirty.

"It's a good thing they stopped you." Oliver cheerfully intoned when no one said anything. The constant questioning of his character didn't seem to faze him. "That was wildfire. Magical flames designed to stop intruders by melting the skin off their bones in seconds."

Callan looked murderous, that signature muscle in his jaw

twitching like crazy. Something told me wildfire would not be enough to stop a rampaging Callan.

"Let's move on, shall we?" Oliver walked us over to the table that held the map, along with a long silver chain holding a clear crystal that hollowed out into a sharp point at the tip. He picked it up gently before turning to me and placing it in my outstretched palm.

"Hold it over the map and let it dangle." I did as instructed, flipping my hand over while grasping the chain so that the crystal hovered above the map, slowly swinging in small circles from the movement. "Now, close your eyes. I want you to concentrate on the person you are trying to find. In this instance, think about the scent that you are hunting. We know the culprit is magically hidden, but you should still be able to pinpoint the witch who cast the spell. Magic is all about intention."

I nodded. I could do this. I had to do this. For Evie.

Closing my eyes, I wracked my brain for a moment before I located the scent Callan had taught me to catalog. It filled my nose, jasmine and blood taking over my senses. The chain vibrated in my hand, subtly at first and then stronger, the spinning intensifying until I was sure it was not my doing.

"Good. Very good, you're a natural." I could hear Oliver's smile but kept my eyes firmly shut, not wanting to disrupt whatever magic I was managing to do. "Now move your arm. Let the crystal guide you. You'll know it when you find it."

Sure enough, I could feel the crystal pulling me in a particular direction. I slowly moved my arm, the vibrations of the chain growing stronger, telling me I was making the right choice. I moved a little bit more, gasping when the crystal surged downward, pulling the rest of me with it as it thudded to a stop on the map before completely going still. I fell backward on my ass, caught off guard by the abrupt movements.

"Ow." I winced as I took Lily's offered hand, pulling me back on my feet. I gave her a thankful smile, cheeks tinged with pink.

"Oh, that'll be fun." Wolfe mused as he looked over the map.

Callan leaned over to see where he pointed before flattening his expression into a grim line. He met my eyes for the first time today, and whatever words I might have been about to say died in my throat, unprepared for the sudden attention. I averted my gaze, internally beating myself up for giving in so quickly.

"Where are they?" Lily asked as she turned away from me and back to the table regarding the spot the crystal had marked. "I don't recognize this place."

Wolfe came around to our side of the table, slinging an arm around both of our shoulders. Callan's eyes narrowed at the movement. "That, my darlings, would be Holes and Poles."

I jerked out from under his touch, confusion across my face. "Excuse me?"

He grinned widely, his grey eyes sparkling with amusement. "Holes and Poles. The finest strip joint in all of the west coast."

"And you would know a lot about that, wouldn't you?" It was meant as a joke, but I wouldn't put it past Wolfe to be a frequent patron of the establishment.

"I've been there once or twice." His smile was positively feral, and I giggled at Lily's eye roll. "If we hurry, we should be able to get there before they close for the night. Might be easier getting information from them if there are innocents around, so they can't attack us."

"You should head back," Callan interjected, his full attention on me. "We don't know what to expect out there. A witch of this caliber will not give up the information easily."

This time it was my turn to roll my eyes, and I steeled myself to meet his gaze, trying to push all thoughts of the night before to the back. "You and I both know I won't do that."

I whipped out my knife, brandishing it back and forth in front of me like a wand. "See, I can take them. No problem."

That got a few smiles from the group, except for Callan, who merely stared back. Statistically speaking, he would have to laugh at one of my jokes. Someday.

"If anything goes wrong," This time, he pinned Lily with his stare, and I saw her visibly swallow. I felt him put a little Alpha emphasis on his next words. "You get her out of there. Immediately."

Lily nodded once, determination in her chocolate eyes. "I won't lose anyone else."

WE MADE IT TO HOLES AND POLES WITH PLENTY OF time to spare, the club still bumping and writhing in the early morning darkness of the new day. I yawned, stretching from the excruciatingly short nap I'd been able to take on the ride over. My stomach grumbled loudly, and I was thankful everyone ignored it. After this, I was forcing a stop at the nearest fast-food restaurant, having not eaten since I'd been at Lily's house what felt like a lifetime ago.

Hopping out of the car, I was glad we didn't look out of place. This was not a high-end club; the siding on the building was in various states of disrepair. A crack and peeling red door stood at the center, a tall bald-headed bouncer sitting on a stool out front, checking IDs and letting people in. As we exited the SUV, we drew more than a few stares, and I shied away from the hungry looks of the waiting patrons as we approached the bouncer.

"Nice try, buddy; the line starts back there." The bouncer sounded robotic, barely giving Callan a second glance as he took the ID of the next person and let them in. Callan stood his ground, staring down the bouncer with his imposing figure.

"Don't make me say it again," the bouncer said as he lumbered off the stool and blocked the entrance. Standing, he was much more threatening, a spider tattoo on his neck coming into full view as he stepped more into the light. Callan didn't seem phased, and I watched as he squared his shoulders and stared the bouncer directly in the eye. I couldn't see his face from where I stood, but the flash of fear on the bouncer was unmistakable.

"You will move," Callan ordered menacingly, making sure to

enunciate every word. I felt the familiar cooling tingle of his Alpha presence.

The bouncer made a wise choice and opted for life, sitting back down and gesturing us inside without another word. We waltzed inside, the scent of sex and booze assaulting my nose. Scantily clad women gyrated on poles all around the room.

I sneezed twice in quick succession, and Callan reached an arm in front of me, halting my path.

"Breathe, concentrate. Catalog the smells and then block them."

"I can block them out?" I asked, sneezing again as the assault continued.

"It's helpful in situations like these. Do what I showed you, only this time, once you've got the scents, block them out. Imagine a wall of sorts between them and your nose. Eventually, you'll be able to pick and choose which scents you want to keep out."

I closed my eyes briefly, identifying the scents and filing them away before I imagined a wall as he said. It wasn't a very good wall, patchy in some spots and not at all something I thought would hold, but when I opened my eyes, I no longer felt the urge to sneeze. A sigh of relief escaped me. Nodding his approval, Callan dropped his arm, and we moved forward towards an eagle-eyed bartender who had his eyes on us the moment we walked in.

"Shifters?" he snarled as we approached, judgment plainly written across his face. I tried to scent him, but my wall had been more effective than I intended as I realized I couldn't smell anything. Definitely something I needed to practice.

"We're looking for a witch," Callan demanded, no pleasantries in sight. The barkeep smirked, his eyes raking over us and hesitating too long on Lily and me for my liking. He was young, barely old enough to be behind the bar, and his cockiness radiated off him in waves.

"Take your pick. This is a witch club, dumbass." A snarl

erupted from Callan, but I stepped forward, placing a hand on his arm with a tight squeeze, urging him to calm down.

"We're looking for a powerful witch. Probably the most powerful one in here." I looked the man over, noticing how his eyes lingered on my chest, and I decided to take a different approach. Straightening my back and jutting my chest out, I leaned over the edge of the bar as close as I could get, widening my eyes to look as innocent as possible. I met his hungry stare, tongue darting out to tease my bottom lip before I gave it a soft bite for maximum effect.

"Could you please point us in the right direction so we can get what we came here for, we'll be out of your hair in no time?" I batted my eyelashes for emphasis, reaching a hand out to rest on his arm. He looked at my hand like he'd been shocked, a blush creeping up his neck.

"You- You want Roxy," he stuttered out and then stood straighter, regaining his confidence. "Straight back, through the VIP section. Tell them Jacob sent you, and they'll let you through. Come see me after for a drink, yeah?"

I smiled demurely, straightening back into an upright position. Turning towards the back of the club, I gave him a nod of thanks as I urged the group to move, walking off in the direction he'd instructed. Lily was smirking, and Wolfe looked like he was holding in laughter, but it was the murderous look on Callan's face that caught my eye.

"What?" I told him as we moved through the crowd of horny men and barely dressed women. "Your way wasn't working."

"I was handling it," he said sourly, his emerald eyes blazing with flecks of gold as we continued.

"Maybe," I retorted, dodging around a red-headed dancer as she gave a man a lap dance. "But my way doesn't involve killing anybody."

This time Wolfe did laugh, trailing behind us as we made our way through the club. "You're an adorable little rabbit. Callan's mad for much more than that."

"What?" I asked, but Callan turned to glare at Wolfe, who quickly shut his mouth, amusement still dancing in his eyes. Wolfe gave me a shrug, and before I could question him more, we pulled to a stop in front of the VIP section. A small, dimly lit room was roped off with another bald-headed bouncer standing guard that looked suspiciously exactly like the one from the front.

"Jacob sent us. For Roxy?" Wolfe said, taking the lead this time with a charming smile to the bouncer. We were met with no resistance, just a non-committal grunt, and we were ushered through, the rope clicking to a close behind us.

As we moved through the room, I realized it was dimly lit for a reason. It was a small circular space with plush velvet couches adorning the edges. It was mostly empty, except for a man in one corner, entertaining two dancers I hoped worked at the club. I say hoped because he had his face buried between the breasts of one girl, while another one was on the floor in front of him, his cock buried deep in her mouth, making loud moaning sounds as she worked his shaft.

"Oh my god," Lily whispered as we averted our eyes, practically running to the small black door hidden in the room's back corner. Once on the other side and the door shut firmly behind us, we erupted into a fit of laughter that bordered on hysterical. Tears leaked from the corners of my eyes as I fought to catch my breath.

"Are you done yet?" A sultry voice emerged from the corner of the room, drying up our laughter immediately. The room had been empty seconds before, but now a large velvet chair, almost throne-like stood at the back, where a woman sat perched on the edge. Her deep ebony hair cascaded around her in curated waves, her espresso skin clear and glowing. A vibrant red slip dress adorned her body. I would have asked her for her skincare routine if I didn't think she had a hand in Evie's death.

"Are you Roxy?" Callan asked, his tone softer than it had been when we'd spoken to the bartender. Either he thought she was extremely attractive, which I would begrudgingly have to agree with, or he was trying not to piss her off. My money was on the latter.

"Who wants to know?" she asked slyly, a calculating look in her frigid brown eyes. As her eyes roamed over us, I felt the gentle whisper of magic sliding over my skin. I looked to my counterparts, but no one seemed to notice.

"I think she's using magic," I whispered out of the corner of my mouth to Callan, who gave me a surprised look but then nodded.

"I am the Alpha of the Clover Pack," Wolfe said as he stood to his full height, towering a few inches even over Callan as he stepped forward. I felt his fiery Alpha power surge as he let some of it pour from him to support his statement. "Someone is murdering shifters, and we know you had something to do with it. Who are you working for?"

Her ruby red lips broke into a smile, her perfectly porcelain teeth shining brightly. "I cannot help you. I know nothing of these murders you speak of."

Lily cocked her head to one side, before letting out a quiet growl. "Lie."

Roxy's smile widened further, but she said nothing. Callan stepped forward, coming to stand alongside Wolfe, his frosty powers permeating around the room, their powers mingling. Together they formed a protective stance in front of both me and Lily. I felt the magic whispering on my skin intensify, until I could almost taste it on my tongue. It felt delicate, fragile compared to the dominating Alpha power I was used to and the electric magic I'd felt from Oliver.

"You will get nothing from me. Leave now." Roxy's voice boomed through the room as she moved to stand to her full height, dress rustling with her movements. "If you leave now, no harm will come to you."

Lily growled louder, the sound reverberating through the space. "Lie."

Roxy threw her head back and chuckled, a sinister glint in her eye as she focused on us. "Oh, you're good. I am so going to enjoy listening to your screams as you die."

"Ignus," she whispered without hesitation, my ears ringing as the entire room exploded and I was launched backward into the wall. I hit with a hard thud, my breath whooshing out of me instantly. All around me, I heard growls and snarls, and it was a few moments before my shifter healing kicked in, knitting my hearing back together and clearing the spots from my eyes. A solid pulse set in the back of my head, but I had no time to worry about that now.

Looking around, I seemed to have been forgotten. Wolfe and Callan stood in a standoff across from Roxy, the only sign that the blast had affected them being the burning holes in their clothes, the skin underneath raw and pink but otherwise healed. Lily was recovering just as I was, only a few feet away, blood dripping from her nose. Their Alpha powers must have made them less vulnerable to whatever the hell she had done. Bouncing back quickly, Lily extended her claws, standing in a protective gesture in front of me, backing me towards the door for a quick exit if things went south. Well, further south.

As I watched, Callan extended his claws, and I could see a purple haze take form, coating the razor-sharp edges. His powers, I realized. Wolfe, on the other hand, went full shifter, transforming into his even bigger bear form, clothes ripping to shreds as he changed in the blink of an eye. A fiery halo appeared, coating his skin from head to toe. Together they moved, charging straight for Roxy.

They moved as a well-practiced unit, clearly having fought together before. Callan lashed out at Roxy, swiping at her with his claws. With another mumble under her breath, she disappeared, reappearing a few feet behind Callan, but Wolfe was already there, and he swiped with his gigantic bear claws. She moved fast, but not fast enough. Wolfe's claw caught her shoulder, eliciting a loud cry of pain as she moved away.

"Scutum!" she shouted as a large shield appeared before her, closing her off into the corner she stood. The familiar tingle of her power built in the air, running along my skin, and I watched as Callan and Wolfe advanced on her position, unaware of the blast she was powering up. I noticed small golden threads begin to weave out from her, creating a lattice effect over most of the room. She was huddled in her corner, trying to look as small as possible, but I saw the evil glint in her eye. She would kill us all if I didn't stop her.

I pushed my way around Lily, desperate to warn them, elbowing her hard in the stomach when she tried to stop me. If I could get the guys under the lattice, they might be able to dodge the worst of it.

"Get down! She's going to blow up!" I screamed at them, realizing my mistake as soon as both men turned their attention to me and away from her. Roxy's eyes landed on me, and a triumphant look stretched across her face.

"Ignus!" she screamed, throwing her hands out in front of her. I had just enough time to shove Lily to the ground hard, well under the lattice above us, before ducking down myself. My hunch proved right as I watched each golden thread explode where it stood, louder and stronger than before, searing droplets of heat burning as it landed. Stars danced across my vision as my ears rang, and my only hope was that Callan and Wolfe had dropped in time.

Sudden smoke obscured the room, and I coughed, lungs burning as I fought for air. I frantically searched around for Lily, but she was no longer where I'd left her, having been separated from each other during the explosion.

"Lily?" I choked out, barely hearing over the ringing in my ears. Coughing again, I stumbled to a stand, a shriek escaping me as red-taloned nails gripped my arms tightly, piercing through my jacket and into my skin below. Roxy swam into view, a twisted expression marring her perfect face. I struggled, trying to reach for my knife in its sheath, but the more I struggled, the weaker I became. I looked down at the hands around my arm, dread filling me as I saw the thin golden threads of power that coated her fingers. The strength fled my body, the edges of my vision swimming, darkening into nothing as I lost consciousness.

"Sleep, Filia. Your misery will be over soon."

Chapter Twenty-Three

The cage I awoke in was my least favorable outcome of the day. It was barely bigger than a shoebox, with only a small cot and a metal bucket in one corner. The smell of sweat and feces permeated my nose as I sat up groggily, making me gag. I tried to catalog the scent before I realized I couldn't. A sharp twinge of pain in my arm startled me, and I looked down, realizing my arms were still punctured from where Roxy had dug into them. Was I not healing? I concentrated hard, urging my body to shift, but nothing happened, not even a twitch.

"Oh no," I whispered out loud, despair creeping in as I realized I was powerless and trapped. This wasn't supposed to happen. We were just supposed to find the witch, get her to give up her client, and then I'd be then thousand dollars richer. Where was everyone else?

I ran to the bars of my cell, jumping back as I felt the zap of electricity shock me when I touched the bars. Frowning, I touched them again, but there was no pain. Why did they have me in an electrified cell that didn't even hurt?

Shaking my head, I ran to the side of my cell, taking stock of the room beyond. I wasn't the only cell here. Four other cells stood alongside mine. Standing on my tiptoes and craning my neck, I saw that only the cell next to me was occupied, and not by one of my friends.

The prone figure faced away from me, sleeping on the cot. There were no blankets in sight, only a pillow that looked more like a piece of paper than a sleeping device. I couldn't see his face, just a mop of unruly sandy blonde hair and obvious malnourishment being my only clues to his identity. His clothes were disgusting and tattered, and I wouldn't be surprised if those were the clothes he'd come in here with.

Aside from him, the room was empty. Each cell was padlocked shut, with no hope of getting it open without any abilities. I doubt I could, even if I had my shifter abilities. Rabbits didn't come with any extra strength, but at least I might be able to squeeze myself through the bars. I closed my eyes and tried again, growling in frustration when nothing happened—time to try another approach.

"Hey!" I hollered, boring a hole with my stare in the back of my prison mate's head. When I received no response, I picked up the metal bucket, thankfully empty, and banged it on the bars of the cage. "Hey! Hello! Earth to prisoner!"

"Did they put you in here to irritate me to death?" A gravelly voice came from the man, and I watched in satisfaction as he sat up gingerly in his cot, turning to face me with a death glare. He stood, and I noticed how tall he was, towering over me by at least a foot. He was impossibly thin, cheeks gaunt, and face riddled with so many scars it was hard to look at him. His brown eyes were dull, and he averted them from mine every time I tried to catch them.

"Who put us here?" I asked him softly. I'd also be snappy if I were in the same state as him. He observed me for a moment, then shrugged his shoulders.

"I stopped asking a long time ago."

"How long have you been in here?" I questioned, hoping to get enough information from him to help us get out of there. He pulled up his left sleeve, studying something on his arm before he turned back to me, face devoid of emotion and his eyes trained to a spot beyond my head.

"Seventy-seven days," he said, holding his arm up so I could see. I covered my mouth in horror as I saw the markings. He had rows and rows of thin slash marks from wrist to elbow. The ones closest to his elbows were scabbed over, the wounds becoming increasingly swollen and fresh as they went on. Some of the ones closest to his wrists still oozed blood, and my heart ached for him and the pain he must have endured.

"They tell me when they run out of space, they'll slash my wrists and put me out of my misery," he said dully, regarding the wounds on his arm like it was a science project.

"Fuck that," I told him fiercely. "I'm getting us out of here."

He barked a laugh, sharp and soulless. "Good luck with that. Once they get what they want from you, they'll kill you. You are not the first person to occupy that cell."

"And what is it they want from you?"

He met my eyes for the first time, and even in his emaciated state, I could see the intelligence that lurked beneath the surface.

"Something I am unable to give," he expressed finally before lying back down on his cot and turning away from me, ending the conversation.

"Would you at least tell me your name?" I asked in frustration. If I was going to get out of here, I needed all the information I could get. The silence was my only answer.

I huffed, pacing around my cell. He might be willing to give up, but I would never give someone the power to break my spirit. If they wanted to kill me, then fine, but I wouldn't sit in this cell and waste away like this guy. I'd play it smart, biding my time until I could fight tooth and nail for my freedom.

What about Callan? And my friends? I hoped they would come for me, but I'd be surprised if they even knew where I was. Or if they were even alive. I pushed that thought out of my mind. There's no way some raging bitch witch had taken down two Alphas of the Clover pack. She'd caught us off guard, that's for sure, but it'd take more than a couple of explosions to take them down.

No, they were out there somewhere, hopefully searching for me. But I couldn't put all my eggs in one shifter basket. It had been hard enough to track down the witch in the first place, and without my ability to find the scent, I don't know if they'd be able to find me, wherever I was.

I was on my own.

THEY CAME FOR ME A FEW HOURS LATER WHEN I WAS starting to debate eating the bars of my cell to fill the hole in my stomach. I don't know how long I'd been knocked out, so I could only assume it had been well over twenty-four hours since I'd eaten last.

My prison partner was less than helpful about feeding times, saying they only fed us when they remembered to. That wasn't going to fly with me.

Two men opened the lone door of the room, coming to a halt in front of my cell. They were each dressed in combat gear, large military-grade rifles held in their hands. They both rocked identical buzz cuts and blank stares. I looked at them side to side, realizing they were, in fact, the same person.

"Are you twins?" I blurted out. They stared at me blankly as if they had no idea what I was saying. "Anybody home in there?"

"They aren't twins," Scarface said from his permanent place on his cot. Scarface wasn't the nicest name I could have come up with, but he hadn't given me much to go on. "They're magical apparitions. They do the witch's bidding."

"The witch? Do you mean Roxy?" He lifted one shoulder, giving me a pained grimace as he did.

"The witch who brought you in. Black hair, quite pretty," I rolled my eyes hard. He was too depressed to help me escape, but he had time to think the witch was pretty?

"Wait, you saw her bring me in?"

"Yeah. That's how she does it. She just appears in a cell with someone and then disappears. That's the only time I see her."

"She must still be here if her magic pets are still around." I wasn't sure that's how it worked, but I'd bet my left hind foot she was still nearby. Scarface only shrugged, turning back to face away on his cot.

The last thing I'd do before leaving this place would be to hunt her down and slit her throat. I felt heat charge my body as I held on to my anger, comforted by its warm embrace.

"Step away from the bars." A dull, monotone voice came from Thing 1 while Thing 2 stood by.

"And if I don't?" I retorted. Not sure what arguing with a fake person would do for me, but I didn't have a compliant bone in my body.

Thing 2 raised his machine gun, pointing it straight at me. I heard the click of the safety as he prepared to fire. I bit my tongue, holding back the next smart comment I had loaded. Escaping would be a lot harder if I was dead. I threw my hands up in a placating gesture, backing away from the cell door.

"Arms out in front of you," Thing 1 continued. As soon as I put my arms out, Thing 1 approached, swiftly clicking a pair of cold metal cuffs around my wrists as I stared at the barrel of the rifle. A small beeping sounded as the lock clicked in place on the cuffs. Gripping the metal between my hands, Thing 2 ushered me out of the cell.

The second I was out, I tried to shift. If I could turn into my rabbit, I was sure I'd be able to hide and dodge my way to safety. It was a lot harder to catch a tiny target. Dismay washed over me when nothing happened, and the cuffs made much more sense. They were dampening my abilities while I was out of the cell. Fuck.

At the prodding of the rifle in my back, they led me out of the room, and I got my first glimpse of what lay beyond my prison. It wasn't what I expected. We stood in an enclosed room with no other doors besides the one we'd come through, with barely enough room to fit all three of us. The walls and door behind us were painted completely white, with no labels or tags in sight. As the door closed behind us, two other doors opened, one to the left and one to the right. The Things ushered me through the left one, where we were met with an identical room to the one we'd just come through. This time, we took a right.

We continued through the maze of rooms, each new room that opened a mirror image of the one we'd just come through. I tried to keep track as we went, but after the first dozen, I couldn't remember it anymore. We walked for what felt like an hour before we finally opened a door into a room with only one carob-stained door directly adjacent to where we'd entered.

We stepped inside, and I blinked at the sudden lack of light compared to the brightly lit hallways we had just traipsed through. We were in a modest dining room, a long ivory table spanning the length of the rectangular space. The deep red of the walls and the lack of windows made the room feel smaller than it was, the only lighting emanating from a few lanky candles adorning the table.

Only three chairs were placed at the table, two of them already filled. My blood boiled when I saw Roxy sitting across from the one empty seat, wearing a self-satisfied smirk as she watched me. I'd like to see if she could still smirk when I got my hands around her throat.

Next to her sat a woman I had never seen before. She was beautiful, or at least she had been. Before the giant scar that decorated her face, one angry gash ran diagonally from the corner of her forehead, not stopping until the end of the opposite cheek. A redhead, her curls flowed wildly at all angles, a caricature of Medusa. She met my stare; her one good baby blue gave a new meaning to the term crazy eyes.

"Rowan, how nice of you to join us," Roxy quipped, her once honeyed voice sounding like nails on a chalkboard. She gestured to the seat across from them. "Take a seat, have a bite to eat. You must be starving."

When I didn't move, Thing 2 jammed the rifle into my back, reminding me that I didn't have a choice. Begrudgingly I approached, sliding into the seat after another friendly display of aggression from my mindless friend.

I reviewed the plate in front of me, unable to stop the bit of drool that escaped me when I saw the enormous slice of roast beef in front of me, along with peas and carrots and a huge helping of mashed potatoes.

"Hungry?" Roxy taunted. "Dig in."

"I'm not eating this. How do I know you haven't poisoned it?" I was hungry, but I wasn't stupid enough to dive headfirst into a pit of lava.

"If we wanted to kill you, we'd have done so already," Roxy said snidely. I stared her down for a moment, contemplative. She was right. I'd been completely at their mercy this whole time; she'd had me unconscious for who knows how long. What gain would she get bringing me here, to poison me while I ate? I needed all the strength I could get if I was going to get out of here alive.

After another moment of hesitation, I picked up my fork awkwardly in my cuffed hands and dove in. The roast was deliciously tender, and the veggies were salted to perfection. I may have had a mini orgasm at my first bite of potatoes. The girls watched me as I ate shamelessly, not speaking until I'd polished off the last bite of beef. I downed the glass of water that magically refilled before finally wiping my face off and returning their stairs.

"Why am I here?" Hostility dripped from my every word.

"We can do this the easy way or the hard way," Roxy said, and I cackled loudly.

"What are you, a tv movie cop?"

Her hands slammed on the table, the plates rattling with the movement. I jumped, not expecting the sudden outburst. "Do you think this is a game, Rowan?"

"I don't know what this is!" I shouted back at her, letting my frustration burst out with my words. "Are you the one who has been killing innocent shifters? Innocent children? We thought you were hiding them, but maybe it was you this whole time?"

The scarred companion giggled, a wild, manic sound, the first she'd made since I sat down. She wrung her hands together, an almost obsessively anxious movement. I forced my eyes back to Roxy.

"You don't understand." Roxy sighed. "Any soul should be honored to be chosen as a sacrifice to Queen Tantaii."

"Excuse me? Are you telling me you killed all those innocent people as a sacrifice to some deity?" My vision swam red as the weight of their words dawned on me. "You killed my friend as a sacrifice?"

"No, no. Not that one." The crazy lady murmured as she started to rock back and forth slightly.

"Lexi, shut up," Roxy directed, but it was already too late. At the sound of her name, she snapped her head up, her good eye trained on me as she went completely still. When she spoke again, her voice was childlike, almost mocking.

"We thought she was you," she said, voice pitching lower as she gave a throaty chuckle. "Oops."

Her giggle dried up in her throat as I launched myself across the table, fingers outstretched towards her neck, even with my cuffs. A blinding white light flashed just as I could feel her skin under my nails, and then everything went dark.

Chapter Twenty-Four

"You sure do sleep a lot," my cellmate from hell mused as he watched me struggle to sit up in my makeshift bed. My head throbbed, the dim light radiating from the singular bulb on the ceiling making my eyes squint in pain as the memories of what happened returned to me.

"Get fucked," I grumbled, not in the mood for his snide remarks over the pounding in my head. A faint chuckle was my only answer.

I couldn't believe I let that cunt Roxy get the jump on me. That was twice now she'd kicked my ass, and I hadn't even laid a finger on her. The angry snarl that came out of me shocked even me.

"That bad, huh?" I squinted at the thin man across the bars of our prisons. A twinge of pain from my arm made me look down, a hiss escaping me when I saw the angry red slice of skin, a slight halo of blood crusted around the wound. Seeing my look, he raised his arm so I could see the masses of small, thin scars and a glaringly fresh one towards the skin of his wrists. "Been there, done that."

"What's your name?" I finally asked. He considered me for a moment before responding.

"Most people call me Cas."

"Most people?" My hair tickled my shoulder as I cocked my head to the side.

"The ones who don't are dead." He bared his teeth at me, a failed attempt to look threatening. I was sure I could break him in half with just one hand.

"Are you a shifter?" I highly doubted it. He didn't look like one of us. There was a certain quality every shifter had, I'd come to realize. A calculating, predatory glint in the eyes that Cas didn't have. A certain way that we moved. He was intelligent, I could see it in his every movement, but he was not a shifter.

He laughed, a dry condescending sound. "Don't be ridiculous."

"Then what are you?"

His eyes shifted to the side briefly before they landed back on me. "I do magic."

Ah. A witch. That made much more sense.

"What'd you do to get landed in here?" I shifted into a stand, trying to relieve the soreness the makeshift cot was causing me.

"Take your pick. I've committed more crimes in my life than I have good deeds." He wasn't ashamed of it, quite the opposite. An air of arrogance surrounded him.

"But what did you do to piss Roxy off?"

"Roxy?" A smarmy smirk spread across his face. "She's not in charge here."

"Oh right," I recalled what she had said at the dinner table, and my anger rose again, Evie's lifeless form flashing across my mind. "She said something about sacrificing to a Queen. Titania? Tatiana?"

"Tantaii," Cas interrupted, narrowing his eyes at me.

"Right, that!" I snapped my fingers, giving him a nod. "Who is she, and why is she killing people?"

"You don't know anything, do you, little rabbit?" His eyes were condescending, tone flat. "If you don't want to end up like me, you should give them what they want."

"Why haven't you?"

I threw my hands up in frustration. "I don't even know what they want!"

"If you stopped attacking every five seconds, we could talk about it." Roxy's sultry voice floated from the opposite side of the cell, and I almost jumped out of my skin, not realizing she'd entered. Teleporting bitch.

"I won't apologize for standing up for my friends." I glared back, trying to burn a hole in her head.

"I'd expect nothing less from you. Come with me," she said, before disappearing into thin air.

I looked around in confusion. How did she expect me to follow her? A few seconds passed, and my best friends Thing 1 and 2 came through the door. I dutifully put my arms out in front of me. I hated being confined, but I needed answers. The more information I had, the easier it would be to make my escape when the time was right.

A few seconds later, we exited, and I was again led through the endless maze before stopping in front of the final door. This time when we entered, the room was arranged to look completely different.

Instead of the dining table I had launched myself over, there was only a small metal chair in the center of the room. A large square of thin plastic lay beneath the chair, a tray with multiple scary-looking tools next to it. Roxy stood to one side, face grim. Lexi stood to her right, her bright blue eyes sparking with mirth.

Roxy lifted one slim arm and snapped, the sound echoing loudly in the silent room. The Things pushed me to the chair, widening my cuffs and fastening them around each armrest. They followed suit with my legs, and seconds later, I was trapped. I glared at Roxy.

"You understand, of course. Last time we let you free, you attacked." Roxy's haughty tone made me want to rip her vocal cords out with my bare teeth.

"Let me out of this, or I'm going to-"

"What are you going to do?" She looked down her nose at me, and Lexi shifted anxiously, not saying a word.

"What do you want from me?" I gritted out. Submission was against my nature but strapped down to this chair, I had no other choice.

"See, now that wasn't so hard, was it?" Roxy laughed as I tried to lunge out of my chair, a squeak of surprise coming out of Lexi. She backed away slightly.

"We need your help." Roxy approached the chair, crouching down to be at eye level with me. Her perfectly flawless skin made me want to gag.

"If you wanted to ask for my help, there are much better ways to do it."

"You wouldn't have helped us." she said with finality.

"You don't know that," I argued. "You don't even know me."

Roxy raised her brows, a challenge in her eyes that I couldn't help but reciprocate. "You would have helped us if we came to you, told you we murdered three shifters and ripped out their hearts as a sacrifice to Queen Tantaii, and we need your help to resurrect her?"

I spluttered, eyes widening before I schooled my expression, hardening the walls around my heart. I wouldn't let these people see me cry.

"Who is Queen Tantaii, and why do you need me to help you? And where are my friends?" They could have told me it was a world-ending apocalypse, and I still wouldn't help them, but the more information I had, the better. Callan would want to know everything I could find out if I ever saw him again. I didn't even know if my friends were alive or dead.

"Now you are asking the right questions." Roxy gave me a nod of approval before moving to stand at her full height. I had no doubt it was so that she could look down on me.

"Do you believe in fairies?"

I shook my head like a wet dog, trying to clear my ears because I must have heard her wrong.

"Did you say fairies?" I couldn't stop the incredulous look on my face. "Like the sprightly little creatures? Have wings, sprinkle fairy dust, steal your gold coins?"

She rolled her eyes, sharing an amused look with Lexi. "You have so much to learn, Rowan."

"Look, two weeks ago, I had no idea shifters even existed. If you told me fairies were real, I'd believe you."

"The fairies that you know of do not exist. No tiny creatures are flying around stealing your gold."

"Okaaaaaaay," I said, urging her to continue.

"But fae do exist. The fae are a powerful master race of magical beings. They were born of Faerie, the fae realm, where they've always resided. Until now."

I stayed silent, listening. Something told me I would not like where this was headed, but I was about to get some real information for the first time in two days. Lexi moved then, standing next to Roxy with her chaotic gaze locked on me.

"Queen Tantaii is the Fae monarch. Or was. Cursed by an usurper for the last five hundred years, confined to a prison between our realms."

"I'm waiting for the part where this has anything to do with me." My patience was growing thin, the hard metal of the chair biting into my tailbone. "Sounds like she is where she belongs."

Lightning quick, Lexi's hand slapped across my face as hard as she could. Pain blossomed on my cheek.

"You will respect the Queen," Lexi commanded, her voice deeper than it should have been.

The metallic taste of blood pooled on my tongue, and I spit it out, aiming as close to their feet as I could.

"We need you to cast the spell to free her from her prison."

I threw my head back as much as I could and laughed, putting extra oomph into it for good measure. "You are barking up the wrong tree. I don't do magic. Here's a thought, maybe you should cast it if you're so powerful?"

Roxy scoffed, arms folding across her chest. "I can't."

I lifted one shoulder as high as the cuffs would let me. "I don't see how that's my problem."

"The curse is very specific. It must be cast by someone born of both realms." She sighed deeply as if explaining this to a toddler. "And the blood of the Monarch."

I stared at her, doing my best not to connect the dots. If I didn't understand what she said, then it didn't need to be true. I could avoid it, the same as I did all my problems. I closed my eyes as she said the words I didn't want to hear.

"You are the daughter of Queen Tantaii, and we need you to set her free."

Chapter Twenty-Five

"Can I have some of the drugs you're on?" I told Roxy to fill the silence in the room. "Reality has been a little too much for me lately."

"Whether you believe it's true or not, you will cast this spell for us," she muttered, shaking her head in disgust as she looked at me. "For the good of your people."

"My people?" I snarled, mirroring her expression with my own. "Whoever these fae are, they aren't my people. I found my people the day I was attacked and left for dead on the side of the road."

The conviction behind my words was genuine.

"I won't help you," I said firmly. "Whoever you think you found, you haven't. The only thing magic about me is that I shift. And not even into a cool lion or a ferocious bear. No, I'm a harmless little rabbit."

"Clearly, the Queen had terrible taste in men," she replied with disdain.

"I knew it from the night I tasted you. Delicious," Lexi's voice wavered slightly as she spoke. Her tongue darted out to slide over her lips, eyes focused on me. "You also zapped me. Bzz!" She poked her finger out quickly, like a bolt of lightning.

"I didn't..." I trailed off, trying to fit together the pieces of that night. Try as I might, I couldn't remember much of what happened. Flashes of rain, the sound of crunching metal. Then nothing. "I can't remember."

Lexi giggled, high-pitched. Roxy placed a warning hand on her shoulder, but she let her continue. This woman had lost a few marbles, clearly unhinged. "We've been looking for you for years."

I said nothing, afraid that interrupting her villain monologue would bring the information train to a screeching halt.

"You wouldn't have died. I was trying to bring you back with me, but then it was like you stole all the light from the sky." She looked up at the ceiling as if she could see through walls, tears slipping down the corner of her eyes. Then she snapped her neck forward, eyes back on me. Accusation filled them, tear streak remnants carving a path down her cheeks. "And stung me with it."

As she said it, the flashes in my head grew stronger until a hazy memory resurfaced. The rain, the car crash, the wolf. And then a buzzing buildup, an electrifying explosion that saved my life. My explosion. Emerald eyes that I now recognized as Callan's looking down on me.

"We found the potion." Roxy interrupted my thoughts, sliding the small thin vial from the front pocket of her fashionable burgundy blazer. I looked down at my chest, shocked. I'd almost completely forgotten about it in all the chaos. "And you're going to take it. The spell won't work if your fae side is still blocked."

"That's why you tied me to this chair? Jesus, I thought you were going to torture me."

She approached me confidently, the potion dangling at her fingertips.

"You'll have to kill me first," I hissed at her, trying to move my face away as she gripped my chin. She muttered something too fast for me to understand, and I felt invisible hands grab my head, pulling it all the way back. Roxy gripped my chin hard until I opened my mouth, pouring the silver potion down my throat. I coughed, trying to fight it, but an even harder pinch forced me to swallow. As soon as I did, all hands let go, freeing my head, and I slumped forward, everything going black.

THE BURN STARTED IN MY CHEST UNTIL IT CAME TO A pool in my stomach, waking me up. My skin itched, then burned all over, and I whimpered from the pain, clenching my eyes shut. It built until I thought I might scream, and then my body went numb. I panted for a few seconds before opening my eyes slowly and taking in my surroundings.

"So? Do you feel any different?" Roxy's irritating voice punctured through the haze, and I opened my eyes.

"No," I lied. I looked around the room, trying to keep the awe off my face. Everything looked brighter and more focused. Roxy looked at me suspiciously, and I tried not to look at the golden threads of magic that wrapped around her skin like vines. Was this what all witches looked like?

I couldn't deny that something had just happened. I looked down at the cuffs, wondering how I could see magic with these on. Maybe they didn't work on the fae side of me? I squinted, looking inside of me to see if any lightning powers were hiding in there, but nothing happened.

"She's lying," Lexi supplied helpfully, her head cocked towards me, listening to my heartbeat. Bitch.

"Perfect." Roxy heaved a triumphant sigh. "Now, will you do the spell?"

"Nope," I huffed. "Can I go home now? It's past my bedtime. They'll be looking for me."

"No one is looking for you," she said snidely. "And even if they were, they couldn't reach you here."

I didn't want to ask, but I had to know. "What do you mean?"

"Your friends are alive. I can't teleport more than one person at a time," she said it sourly, disappointed in the limitations of her powers. "We're not in our realm or the faerie realm. We're in the in-between."

My eyes widened as I looked around the room. I sniffed the air with my human nose but only smelled the faint scent of my sweat. It'd been a few days since I'd had the opportunity to shower.

"Time passes differently here in the in-between. Each day here is about a week in your time."

"A week!?" I groaned, realizing now more than ever that I was alone. "How many days have I been here?"

"Three. You sleep a lot."

"Knocking me out doesn't count as sleeping," I spat. She only shrugged.

"If you won't help us, I have no choice but to leave you with Lexi." She looked almost reluctant to do that, and the look of glee in Lexi's eyes made me shiver.

"Do whatever you want to me. It's not going to make me do anything." Now that I knew my friends were safe, they had nothing over me besides my life. There was no way in hell I was letting some crazy powerful Queen out of her prison, whether she was my mother or not.

Roxy gave me one last look before nodding to Lexi. She muttered something under her breath, and then she was gone, teleporting to wherever her evil lair was. Lexi turned to me, a sinister expression on her face.

"I've been waiting for this moment," she said as she approached the small table next to me, perusing the selection until she found the tool she wanted, a sharp-looking surgical scalpel. My breath caught in my throat as I tried to brace myself for what would come. She bent down next to my head, so close I could feel the tickle of her ragged breathing on my ear.

"You smell like him," she whispered so softly I wouldn't have heard it if she wasn't so close.

I looked at her, confused but had no more time to think as she took the scalpel, slicing it across my arm to join the slash I already had from the previous day. Two more times, I bit my tongue at the pain, unwilling to give her the satisfaction of hearing me cry out.

She looked at me expectantly, and I mustered my fiercest glare, doing my best to ignore the pain in my arm.

"Is that all you got?" Maybe I shouldn't be egging on the psycho torturer but strapped down helpless to this chair, my attitude was my only defense.

"Oh baby, we're just getting started." Putting the knife down, she picked up another contraption that looked suspiciously like a Taser. "If you want me to stop at any time, don't worry. I won't."

"Fuck. You." I gritted through my teeth.

"I was hoping you'd say that," she said before she thrust the Taser at me, and I exploded with agony.

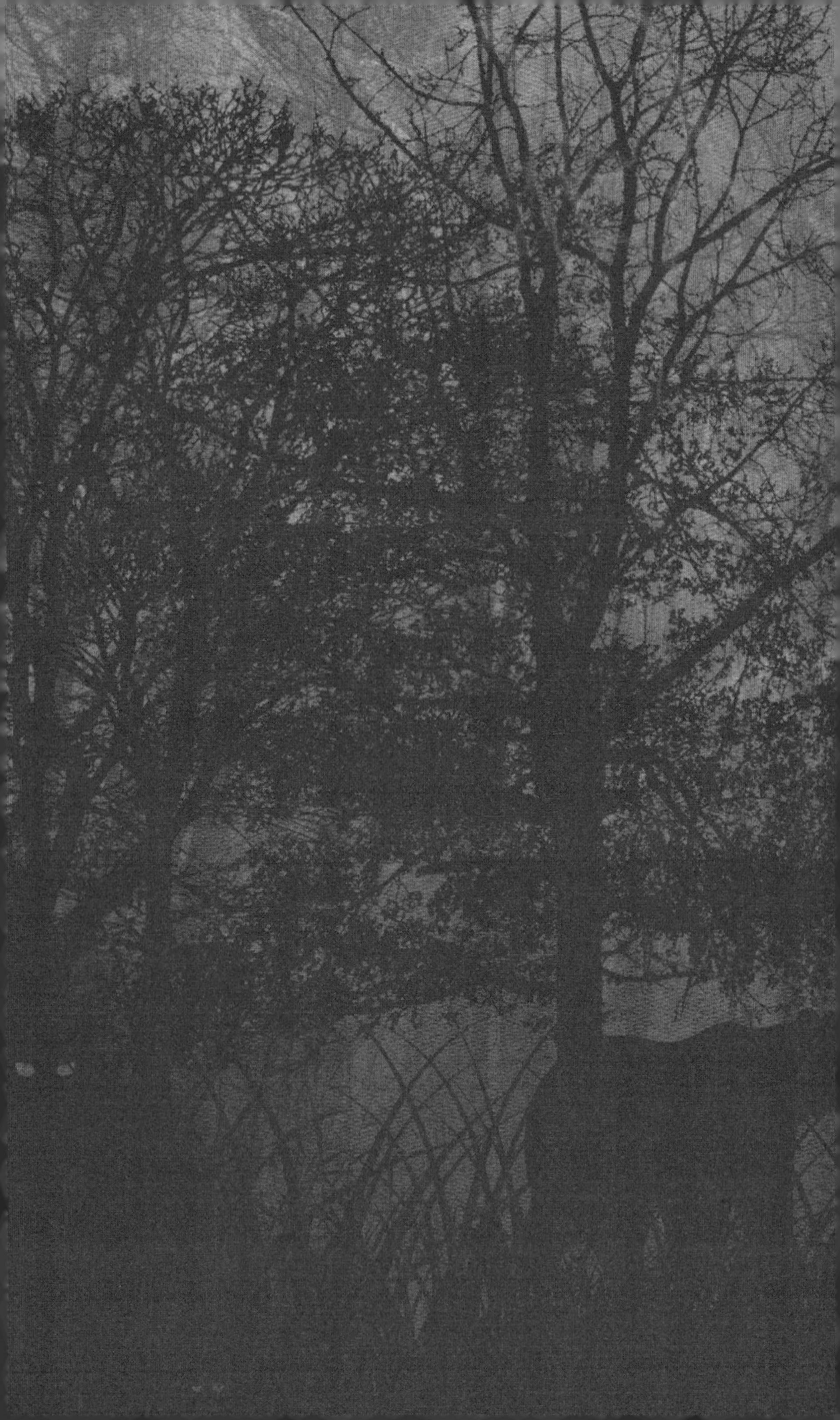

Chapter Twenty-Six

Hours later, I was returned to my cell, unceremoniously tossed on the bed as the door clicked shut behind Thing 1 as he left the room. I looked towards Cas, but it was silent aside from the soft sounds of him breathing. Sleeping, I assumed. I groaned softly as I turned over, trying not to get blood everywhere, but I was fighting a losing battle.

Lexi had more than had her way with me. I had cuts all over my arms and my face, small thin cuts that were too shallow to be serious but big enough to hurt. My ribs and shins throbbed, bruises already forming from where she had kicked me numerous times. I counted myself lucky that nothing felt broken. Small red marks peppered my skin from the multiple Taser attacks.

By the time she called it quits, we were both exhausted, the only thing keeping me conscious was the fiery hatred I had for her. One day, I would kill her. Even if it was the last thing I ever got to do.

Finally, back in my cell, I let the silent sobs wrack my body as I grieved for myself, tears slipping from the corners of my eyes and stinging the cuts on my cheeks. I talked a big game, but I don't know how many more torture sessions I could take.

I didn't want to help them. Logically I knew there had to be a reason Queen Tantaii had been cursed. Even if she was my mother, that didn't mean I owed her anything. I didn't even know her.

What mattered to me was getting out of this hellscape and back to my friends. Forget the ten thousand dollars, I just wanted to still be alive at the end. The Queen could stay in the dirt where she belonged. I couldn't sit on my ass and feel sorry for myself any longer, I had an escape to plan.

"Cas?" I whispered into the dark room. No response. Clearing my throat, I tried again, louder this time. "Cas, wake up!"

"Mmgggmmffhh." He groaned from his cot, the sleep heavy in his voice.

"Wake up!" I hissed at him, trying not to speak too loudly in case someone was standing guard outside. "Do you want to get out of here or not?"

That did it. He sat up and walked towards the bars that joined our cells, and I followed suit. Standing was a little too much for me, so I motioned for us to sit, gingerly lowering myself to the floor with only a small grunt of pain.

"They did a number on you," he observed, his brown eyes tracing the pattern of cuts that adorned my face and arms. His expression was blank, almost numb. "Did you give them what they want?"

"Did you?" I retorted, noticing the additional bruising around his eye that hadn't been there the last time I'd seen him. He just stared at me. "Look, I am going to find a way out of here, whether you join me or not, but two people will be a lot easier than just me."

"What do you have in mind?"

I observed him, not sure if I was able to trust him or not. For all I knew, he was in that cell because he was a crazy serial killer witch who ate the hearts of newborn babies. Highly unlikely, but I knew next to nothing about this man. But at this point, I didn't have a choice.

"They want me to cast a spell for them." His eyebrows rose,

but I kept talking. "I'm not a witch, but they say I'm the daughter of some fae Queen that's been imprisoned for hundreds of years. Apparently, I'm the only one who can free her. I need to escape before that happens."

"And how do you plan to do that?" His doubtful look only made me more motivated to get out.

"That's where you come into play. You've been here a lot longer than me. What can you tell me about their defenses? Weak points?"

He contemplated that for a moment before he answered. "The witch has her bodyguards. I haven't seen much besides that. They always stand guard outside the door and never take breaks."

"Then how do we get out?"

He shrugged. "We'd have to fight them."

I ran my hand through my hair, wincing as the strands sliced into the cuts on my fingers. "That's impossible. We can't even get out of this stupid cell."

"We can take them by surprise." A glint of excitement erupted in his dull eyes, and I grew hopeful. "We take them out next time they come for one of us. Can you fight?"

"I can confidently say I have little fighting experience," I told him honestly. "But I can try."

"They will probably come for you first." I nodded. That made sense. I don't know what they wanted from him, but freeing your imprisoned Queen would take priority. "Go for their legs. They have rocks for brains, so if you can catch them off guard, they won't recover quickly. And if you can get out of the bars of this cell, your powers will work. Just don't let them cuff you. The witch will know as soon as you make your move, so we have to hurry."

We stared at each other, the realization of what we were going to do settling in. It was risky, but I'd rather die trying than rot in this cell until I wasted away.

We had no other choice.

It was two days before they came for me again, or at least what felt like two days. It was near impossible to tell time in a windowless room.

I'd just finished eating the meager meal of a stale piece of burnt toast, half a rotten banana, and five raisins they brought to me daily. It was no wonder Cas was so skinny, and I'd already started seeing changes in my body. My dreams were plagued with prime rib roasts and all the carbs a girl could fit in her mouth at once. The only good part of the meal was the full water bottle that I gulped gratefully.

I was coaxing out the last dregs of water when the door opened, and the Things walked in. I shot a sharp look at Cas, making sure he was ready, and he met me with a determined nod. Over the last few days, we'd chatted more, the most I'd heard him speak since I'd been there, and I finally felt like we were forming some semblance of friendship. Sharing trauma can do that to a person.

"Against the wall, arms out," Thing 2 droned as he unlocked and stepped toward my cell. Thing 1 had his rifle trained on me, ready for anything. I looked at Cas nervously as I put my arms out, pointedly looking from the gun to him. I wouldn't be able to do anything if I was just going to get shot.

Thing 2 approached me robotically, stopping in front of me and pulling the cuffs from his belt loop like always. As he was inches away from my wrists, I shot another pointed look at Cas.

"Hey, dumbass!" Cas shouted, taking my hint. Both Things looked towards the disturbance, Thing 1 moving to aim his rifle at Cas as the noise source.

I saw my opportunity and took it. Crouching low, I launched myself forward, wrapping my arms around Thing 2's legs and bringing him down to the ground in a Superbowl-worthy tackle. His head hit the ground with a sickening crunch as he fell back, unmoving. I ripped the gun out of his hands and aimed it at Thing 1. Praying the safety was off, I pulled the trigger, staggering back from the recoil as the bullets ripped into Thing 1's chest. He fell to the ground, dead. Or deactivated. Or whatever the hell happened to magically created buttholes.

"Hurry up! Find the key. We need to get out of here." Cas's voice snapped me back into action, and I reached down, searching through Thing 1's pocket until my fingers connected with the cold metal of the jail cell key. I yanked it out, rushing over and unlocking the cell for Cas.

"Great job. We've got to get out of here. Come, follow me," he said hurriedly as we walked towards the door. As an afterthought, I doubled back, slipping the strap and rifle off Thing 2 and slinging it over my shoulder. A loud sizzling noise sounded, and we turned back to the cells to watch the last of the Things disappear as their bodies burnt into nothingness.

"That can't be good," I said worriedly, looking at Cas. His grim expression said it all.

"Hurry," he said before he reached back and grabbed my hand, pulling me out the door into the beginning of the hallway maze.

"Which way?" I looked around, having no idea where we could go from here, but Cas seemed to have a plan as he trudged through the door on the left.

"Just stick close to me," he urged, choosing door after door as we wandered through the maze. An itch on my arm made me look down, and I breathed a sigh of relief.

"Hey, my cuts are healing!" I told him excitedly. He gave me a brief smile that didn't quite reach his eyes, his overgrown blonde hair draping over one side as he trudged on. His focus stayed on getting us out of there, and I was grateful he'd helped me escape, or I never would have made it through this part. I'd only been through it a couple of times, but he seemed like he had it memorized.

I briefly considered trying to shift into rabbit form, but I'd only done it one time so far, and I didn't see what kind of help a rabbit would be against a powerful witch and a psychotic serial killer. I may be small enough to escape unnoticed, but I couldn't leave Cas here any longer. He deserved freedom too.

We stopped at the final door, the etched wood staring back at us.

"How do we get out from here?" I asked him. Both times I'd come through this door, the room on the other side had been completely different, and I hadn't seen anything that looked even remotely like an exit.

"Listen, Rowan," Cas turned to me, serious. "There is a high likelihood that we will need to fight whoever is on the other side of that door. Are you ready?"

"As ready as I'll ever be," I took a steadying breath, wrapping my hands around the rifle and holding it ready in front of me. Realization hit me, and I caught his arm as he moved through the door. "How are you going to fight?"

He turned slightly, holding up a palm so I could see. A small ball of electricity formed in his hand, writhing and undulating as he held it. The edges were wild, little zaps of electricity trying to escape the form he contained it to. I frowned as I looked at it, something familiar tickling the edges of my mind.

"Are you-" I began to say, but before I could finish, he opened the door, ushering us into whatever lay ahead of us.

Chapter Twenty-Seven

The room was again different this time, nearly empty except for a raised dais in the center. The dais was long and wide, creating a perfect circle in the center of the room. Three tall platforms stood in a semi-circle around what could only be described as a throne. It was beautiful, the material almost like glass, except in hues of purples, blues, and greens that reflected across the room, creating a dazzling effect of color. The arms of the chair mirrored the body, except for two sharp shards of clear glass that stuck straight up.

Roxy was already there, waiting for us. For me.

"Fuck," I whispered to Cas, inching closer to him as I held my rifle in front of me. "What do we do?"

"We fight," he said, turning to me with a smirk. Before I could react, he lifted his palm, the ball of lighting reappearing. He threw it at me, hitting me right in the chest. The strap of the rifle snapped, and it clattered to the floor as I was thrown across the room from the force of the blast. I hit the wall with a thud, the wind knocked out of me. I gasped around the pain, trying to regain my bearings as I looked at Cas with confusion.

As I watched, his form began to swirl and change, morphing into someone that looked both familiar and alien to me. His dirty blonde hair lengthened, coming to a halt well past his shoulders. His face was elongated, nose sharp, with cheekbones that would make a supermodel envious. His ears thinned to a point, giving him an elfish look while his body filled out, no longer emaciated and wasting away. Most notable were the layers of scars that used to be there but were no longer, leaving him looking entirely unscathed.

Brown eyes that previously had been dull now sparked with the promise of pain.

"Hello, sister."

My eyes widened in shock as I looked him over. The blonde hair and the brown eyes were the same color as my own. I knew now why the lightning was so familiar to me. It was mine. The memory of the night of my attack came rushing back to me, the build-up of heat within my body before I'd blasted Lexi with lightning—my fae powers.

A shimmer began in the air near Roxy, obscuring a large rectangular form. As it went on, the shimmer solidified until I could blink it away, revealing a large iron cell like the one I'd been held in. Tears sprung to my eyes when I locked gazes with familiar emerald ones.

Callan, Lily, Wolfe, and Oliver stood trapped inside the cell. My heart swelled at seeing my friends, even under the circumstances. Everyone in that cage was more powerful than me, a lowly half-breed rabbit shifter with no idea how to control either side of her heritage.

Aside from how incredibly furious Callan looked, they looked relatively unharmed, which was a feat. If that cage didn't block magic, I was sure his eyes would have been completely molten. The other three gave him a wide berth as he paced back and forth, periodically growling deep in his throat.

It was all my fault they were here, that any of this had ever happened. I should have stayed away while I had the chance. Their lives were more important.

Cas interrupted my pity party, impatience oozing from his every pore.

"I warned you this would happen, Olette." His words were directed at me, although I had no idea who he was talking to. "I told you erasing your memories was a bad idea."

"Who the fuck is Olette?" I looked around the room as if searching for someone.

"You are." He stood to his full height, which was a feat as he towered over my human one in his true form.

"Olette Fairchild, Princess of the Faerie, Daughter of the Fallen Queen." He looked down the bridge of his nose as he added, "half-breed abomination."

I heard Lily gasp, but I didn't look. I didn't want to see their faces as they learned I wasn't one of them, not fully. I kept my eyes on Cas, now knowing I could trust him as far as I could throw him, which would be not at all."

"You went into hiding when Mother was cursed as the only one with the power to lift it. You hid for a long time, but each time I found your trail, getting closer and closer. So you crossed into this world and erased your memories. I don't know which fae helped you with the spells, but when I get my hands on them, I will torture them for the rest of eternity."

"You're lying!" I shouted at him, shakily pulling myself into a standing position.

"You think I don't recognize my own sister?" He approached me, hands relaxed at his sides like he didn't see me as a threat. "I knew from the moment you were born that you would be nothing but trouble. A disgusting abomination. Half light fae, half mutt. And finally, after five hundred years, I've got you in my grasp."

Five hundred years. I didn't believe it. I couldn't. I remembered my childhood, the different foster homes, and the people I'd met, both good and bad. I remembered it all.

"You really don't remember," Cas said as he watched me struggle over his words.

"Enough of the reunion," Roxy shouted, breaking us out of our stupor. "Are we going to do this or not?"

Cas shot her a withering glare, and she shrunk back, a feat I hadn't thought possible for her. It was obvious Cas was in charge and had been in control all along. I'd been fooled.

"As soon as you escaped your cell, your pitiful pack was able to find you, just like we'd hoped." My eyes darted to them, their fury filling the room even with their magic blocked.

"You have to do this, Olette," I winced at the name that wasn't mine. He sneered at me, reaching out to grip my arms in a vice. "And if you don't, I will kill your pack while you watch."

My pack.

I looked from them to him, despair settling in. Oliver and Callan shook their heads no at me, but I looked away. I looked at Lily, her beautifully concerned face focused on me, unshed tears clouding her eyes. Wolfe, who just stared back at me blankly, ready for whatever I chose. But I had no choice, not really. I'd do anything to save these people.

Taking my silence for an answer, Cas took my arms and led me towards the dais, where we ascended a few steps, coming to a halt in front of the throne. He looked to Roxy sharply. "You're sure her fae powers have been unlocked?"

She nodded.

"Yes, she drank the potion. She could see my magic." I internally kicked myself for being too obvious. Besides the magic, I didn't feel any different. Maybe she had made a mistake, nothing would happen, and they'd realize they all just needed a really good psychiatrist.

"Good. Bring the guards and Lexi, we may need backup if this goes south," he ordered her as he pushed me into the throne. It was about as comfortable as it looked, like sitting on an igloo. My ass protested from where the glass came in contact with the tattered jeans I still wore, freezing the skin even through the material.

"I don't think that's such a good idea," Roxy protested, her eye glancing back towards the cage and its prisoners.

"Oh, get over it," Cas hissed through his teeth, the skin in the corner of his eyes scrunching harshly as he glared at her. He reached down, tightening a strap around each of my legs, and for the second time in my life, I was being restrained to a chair that I didn't want to be in. "We need backup."

She hesitated for a moment but then shrugged, lifting her hands to do her muttering. I saw the bands of magic spin around her fingers like she was conducting a swarm of fireflies. A door opened near the one we had come through, and in walked both Things, now newly regenerated, and Lexi, her flaming red curls flowing around her like a halo.

"Lexi?" A cracked, broken sound came from Callan, and it took me a few seconds to realize it was a roar filled with pain and anguish.

She giggled, a girly and flirtatious noise that made my blood boil. "Hey, babe."

Babe? Babe?

I noticed it then, a faintly glowing red thread that thrummed to life between them. It was faded, the color dull and cracked in some places. Some sections of it had become completely black, but still, it stayed connected. For the first time, I believed what they'd been telling me. Even if I couldn't see the thread, I would have known. It was written all over Callan's face.

Lexi was Callan's mate.

Chapter Twenty-Eight

Cas snapped two fingers in my face, and I wrenched my eyes away from Callan, trying to ignore the whirlwind of emotions building inside me. I always knew Callan had a mate, but she was supposed to be dead. Not out in the world murdering innocent shifters, aiding in my kidnapping and torture, and helping a crazy fae prince resurrect his imprisoned mother? What the fuck?

I already hated her, but now it was ten-fold.

"We need to start now," Cas said, pulling my attention back to him. He gripped my wrists, raising them well above the arms of the throne. "Put your hands on the tips of the glass shards. Once the spell starts, it cannot be stopped. And whatever you do, try not to pass out. I know that's kind of your thing, but if you do, the spell won't work."

"How are you going to collect my blood?" I asked as I gently placed the palms of my hands on the two protruding shards. No one answered my question as the second I placed my hands down, an invisible force pulled them down, the glass protruding through the other side of my hands, impaling them. I screamed in pain, my cry echoed by furious growls and shouts from my caged friends.

I expected blood to run down the chair, but instead, the

clarity of the glass faded, turning dark with the essence from my blood. I bit my tongue to hold on to the whimper that threatened to escape me, unwilling to give him the satisfaction.

"Good girl." He patted my head, and I growled, darting my head to try and bite him. He chuckled like I was his cute little dog that did a funny trick. I wanted to wipe the smirk off his face so badly. "Finally, it is time."

He walked over to the round platforms behind the chair, waiving his hands as he went. I couldn't see what he was doing, but the glares of my friends and the twinge of blood on my now functional shifter nose told me everything I needed to know. It was the hearts, three hearts torn from the chest of innocent kids who had their chance at life stolen from them. I'd bet my life on it.

Roxy moved to join him, and together they started chanting the same phrase repeatedly. I strained my ears to hear it, but after a few seconds, a tingling began in my hands, spreading up my arms and throughout the rest of my body. The sensation increased, intensifying until my entire body buzzed, like I was made of electricity. I arched my body up as it consumed me, not caring as the glass cut into my hands further.

"Embrace it, Rowan!" A booming voice barely penetrated through the haze, nagging at my psyche. Oliver. "It will kill you if you don't."

"Shut up!" Lexi snapped before everything washed out, and I was nothing but a ball of raw nerves, a live wire with nothing to ground it.

Home.

"Rowan!" Wolfe's hoarse shout reached my ear, and I bucked hard against the chair as I strained towards it.

Friends.

"I can't lose you too!" Lily sobbed, and I cursed the person that had ever made her sound so sad. "Fight!"

Pack.

"Rowan!" Callan's yell was the loudest voice of all.

I screamed, pushing the energy inside me with all my might. A bright flash of electricity burst into the room, devouring outwards in a perfect circle around me. I felt our enemies blast off their feet, launched in varying directions across the room. The cage that held my friends glowed brightly before the hunger of my power chewed threw it, the bars dissolving as if they'd never been there in the first place.

The entire room rocked, and I felt the dais rumble and crack beneath my feet. The earth started to slide apart, and a hole appeared on the ground, directly in front of where I sat. I struggled against the chair, still somehow strapped down to the throne. As I started to panic, a familiar face swam into view.

"Hey," Callan said, eyes running over me as he tore at the bindings holding my feet. Exhaustion pulled at me, and I stared at him, not quite sure I wasn't just having the longest dream in existence.

"I caught the murderer," I told him stupidly, and he crinkled his eyes at me in the first genuine smile I had seen him give. It was a split second before it was gone, replaced with his usual seriousness. "This is going to hurt."

"What-?" I started, but then I screamed as he yanked my hands off the glass shards of the throne. The pain woke me up, chasing the exhaustion away for the time being as it cleared my head. "Ow, you dick!"

"There she is," Wolfe said with relief, and I noticed them huddled near me. Wolfe and Lily both had their claws at the ready; Oliver stood off to the side awkwardly.

"We need to go," he said worriedly, eyes trained on the ever-expanding chasm opening in the floor.

"No one is going anywhere," Cas said as he approached, Roxy and Lexi at his sides, the Things at their backs.

"She's done with this," Callan said, stepping in front of me protectively. I glared at his back. I had forgotten how overbearing he could be, I could fight my own battles. "Let us leave, and we will spare your lives."

Cas grinned widely, upturning his palms, a ball of perfectly formed lightning hovering in them. "If you want to play, we can play."

A sudden growl burst from the side, and I had just enough time to see a thin streak of red dart out at us, tackling Callan in the side. Lexi. They tumbled together, Callan already having shifted mid-fall into his panther form as quick as a blink of an eye.

Using the distraction, Cas lifted his arm, taking aim at me and launching the writhing ball of power he held toward me. I threw my hands up protectively, not knowing what to do, but I was saved from having to as Oliver darted in front of me, his hands launching up and a wall of fire bursting in front of him.

At least, I thought it was Oliver. The man in front of me stood a few inches taller, but now with elongated ears, a long slim nose, and cheekbones I'd begun to recognize. Fae. He looked like the Oliver I knew but not, his hair long and grey in a braided pattern down his back. He turned to me, and one brown eye winked before he turned back towards his opponent, pushing forward with his own fireballs.

To my left, Wolfe and Lily squared off against Roxy, taking turns darting and lunging at her as she tried in various ways to blast them with magic. She disappeared and reappeared at will, each time slower than the last. With two opponents against her, I could tell she was tiring.

A blast from the cavernous opening in the floor pulled my attention, rocking the earth, my balance stumbling, and I struggled to stay upright. I approached the hole against my better judgment, a presence pulling me towards it. After a few more rumbles, the earth stabilized, the last smattering of rocks falling into the abyss. I got as close as I dared, peering over the edge hesitantly.

A sudden burst of light came through the hole, and I pulled myself back hard, barely avoiding getting my face blasted off. The stream went straight through the roof of the building before settling until I could see the sky outside. Or what should have been the sky. Instead of the dark night, as I expected, the outside was a strange reddish brown haze, not a star or mark in sight.

"Olette," a voice commanded, and I whirled around, my voice catching in my throat.

The woman it belonged to was beautiful, very much bearing the features of the fae. She floated slightly above the ground, with power and elegance exuding in waves. It was almost hard to look at her, like looking at a somewhat older mirror image of myself. My face, only more alien, more ethereal. This was Queen Tantaii, there was no doubt about it.

"Speak!" she boomed, and I jumped in my skin. Her glittering eyes observed me suspiciously, and I stood completely frozen. Her suspicion turned into disgust as she continued to stare. "What have you done to yourself?"

She turned to the room, regarding the scene with disdain. Raising her hands high above her hands, she gathered a ball of pulsating yellow-tinged energy in her hands, twisting and guiding it until it solidified into a crystalline ball. She threw it out, hitting everyone in the room with it besides us.

"Cease!" she shouted, and all bodies halted, stopping in their tracks as they fought their battles. I looked at my friends, seeing them strain as they struggled to fight against the Queen's hold. "This fighting stops now."

"Casimir," she snapped at her son, and he was released from the hold. He loftily pulled his clothes back into place, dusting a piece of singed hair off his shoulder that Oliver had sent his way. "How long has it been?"

"Five hundred years." He bowed his head, a begrudging respect in his eyes. "The usurper will rue the day he ever crossed your favor."

"You are a stupid, petulant child." She directed at him, and he flinched. Even locked in the cell, pretending to look beat up, I'd never seen him look as pitiful as he did now. "You have no idea what you've done."

She waved her hands, everyone rising into the air aside from

Cas and me. Her eyes darkened, and I saw a malicious glint as they started to moan and grunt in pain, her hold on them squeezing them tighter than should be possible.

Desperation flared to life in me. If I didn't do anything, everyone in this room would be killed for nothing.

I dug deep inside of me, praying that the lightning inside would heed my call. It responded like a long-lost love, happily greeting me and scorching through my body like wildfire. I screamed against it, throwing my arms out towards her with all I had, not stopping until she was blasted off her feet, a cry of surprise escaping her. I doubt it did any harm, but it was enough to break her hold on everyone, and the crash of their bodies as they hit the floor was a welcome sound.

"How dare you," Casimir hissed at me, bearing down upon me with his hand already alight. More confident now, I reached for the energy again and smiled when I found it. I was not as helpless as I once thought. I threw it at him, not knowing how to do anything with it besides sending it out as pure raw energy. It caught him by surprise, and I relished the look on his face as I hit him, and he blasted across the room, a sickening crunch as he landed.

I looked towards the Queen, who had recovered, now stalking her way toward me, her fury evident on her face. A sudden boom sounded, the roof collapsing in, right on top of the Queen. I looked around, my eyes landing on Oliver as he winked at me. The only people left standing in the room were my people, all in varying states of injury. Roxy and Lexi were nowhere to be found. Cas had disappeared from the direction I'd blasted him, and I had no doubt Roxy had teleported him out somewhere.

Oliver ran over to me, the rest of the pack following as we regrouped together.

"We have to go," he said hurriedly, weaving his hands back and forth in patterns I didn't understand until a small portal began to open out of thin air in front of us. It continued to widen until I could make out the entrance to the Clover Pack gates on the other side.

"Callan, you first," he urged the now human man through the portal, and I did everything in my power to keep my eyes trained on his face and not his exposed skin below. Callan started to protest until Oliver said, "I need you on the other side to make sure it's safe. She'll be right behind you."

Callan glared at him before cutting his eyes to me. I gave him a reassuring smile, motioning for him to go ahead. He gave Oliver one last glare before he jumped through, and after a few long seconds, I saw his face peering in from the other side.

"All right, the rest of you go," he said, pushing Wolfe and then Lily towards the portal. They jumped through with little hesitation, and just as I moved to follow, Oliver placed a halting hand on my arm.

"If you go with them, they will die." His face was completely stoic as if he hadn't said the most terrifying thing I'd ever heard. "She will never stop coming for you."

"What?" I asked him, trying to shrug him off and follow through to the pack lands.

"There is one thing you must learn about fae, little one," he said, his eyes sharp and intelligent. "We cannot lie. If you follow your friends, they will come for you, and you will die. You are not ready."

I gaped at him, mouth flapping open and closed like a fish. A loud explosion from where the roof had collapsed on the Queen made me jump, and I knew we only had a small amount of time before she bursts back through.

"Come with me. I will teach you, and then you will return. To end this, once and for all."

"To end what?" I said softly, feeling defeated. I felt like a puppet, and everyone could pull on the strings attached to my back.

"The destruction of the realms as we know it," I searched his gaze, finding no hint of deception. He believed in this wholeheartedly.

"Rowan!" Callan's pained shout barely reached me, fluttering through the portal. I stared at them, waiting expectantly for me to walk through, to finally be reunited. But if what Oliver said was true, my presence put them in danger, and I couldn't let anyone else die because of me.

"Let's go," I told him, and he nodded. He clapped his hands shut and the portal closed in an instant. A frustrated scream sounded from the pile of rubble, and I could feel the Queen's power building as she prepared to blast her way out of there.

Oliver wasted no time, weaving his hands around until another portal opened ahead of us. Instead of a familiar landscape, all I saw was darkness. Completely pitch black, I couldn't tell what I was looking at or where I was going. Only the word of Oliver, whom I hadn't even known was a fae until ten minutes ago.

"Go, now!" he shouted, sweat beading on his brow from the effort. "I can't hold this for long."

Taking a deep breath, I braced myself for whatever would be waiting for me on the other side. If it meant keeping my friends safe, I'd do whatever I needed to do.

I stepped into the portal, a scream ripping from my throat as the darkness engulfed me, the cold nothingness swallowing me whole.

Midnight Magic Preview
Chapter One

Holy. Fucking. Shit.
 What did I just get myself into?
Darkness enveloped me as I stepped through the portal, a frigid sensation coursing through me for only a moment before light blossomed again. The feeling vanished as quickly as it came, and I found myself in an entirely new world from the one I had just left. My eyes darted back to where I had just come, locking on Oliver's through the now wavering portal. Panic etched across his face as a deafening blast echoed from his side, the edges of the portal rapidly diminishing as his concentration waned.

"Go, I'll find you!" His voice reverberated through the glimmering haze, sounding more like a ghoulish echo than a man as the portal snapped completely shut, disappearing as if it had never been there in the first place.

I stood slack-jawed, taking in my new surroundings. I craned my neck to gaze at the sky, two colossal moons hanging equidistant from each other. Their azure glow painted everything with an otherworldly hue. The rugged and barren landscape stretched before me, marked by jutting rocks and patches of stone. A gentle mist kissed my skin, and I gasped as I discovered an ocean just a few feet behind me, the rocky area I stood on serving as the shoreline. It was unlike any ocean I'd ever seen, its water a royal plum, eerily still, making no sound. Its surface was like glass, smooth and unmarked. I would have attempted to walk on it if not for the slight waver at the water's edge where it lapped at the craggy beach.

As I stared out at the water, a sense of calm fell over me, when I should have been feeling anything but. The water, the moons - everything about this place should have unnerved me, but it didn't. Instead, it felt oddly familiar, like a case of déjà vu. If what everyone had told me was true, it was familiar; I had been here before. This had been my home at some point.

I hope they're okay. Lily. Wolfe. Callan. My pack. I'd barely met them and yet, it was like I'd finally found a place I'd belonged. At least it was, until I learned I was a halfling faerie shifter with lightning powers, the daughter of a bloodthirsty queen. And again, I found myself on the outside. I had so many questions still left unanswered. Especially for Callan, and his redheaded psycho *mate*.

I shuddered against the thought, snapping my emotional walls back into place as I turned back toward land. I didn't have time to digest anything that had happened in the last few hours, and I especially didn't have time to dwell on the panther shifter that always seemed to make my heart beat faster. Not when I had been dropped into the faerie realm, by myself, completely unarmed if you didn't count the unreliable powers I didn't know how to use, and this shifting I had a hard time triggering. My best bet was to regroup with Oliver as soon as possible. Had he even made it out?

I started walking, needing to find some sort of shelter but knowing I shouldn't stray too far. Oliver said he would find me, and while I still didn't know if I could trust him or if he was even still alive, I didn't have much of a choice. This world was already so unlike my own, and I had no idea what else was in store. What if there was acid rain that fell at a moment's notice? Or giant monsters that liked to eat little rabbit shifters? I would be royally screwed.

I'd wait and hope I didn't come to regret that decision.

As I continued, a large outcropping of rocks swam into view, and I picked up my pace as I eyed the darkening sky. I didn't know what nightfall was like out here, or even if it worked the same as it did back home, but I'd rather be under cover than out in the open like I was now.

My haste was rewarded when a few minutes later, I reached the rocks. It was an impressive formation, the large shapes jutting out in all directions, almost throne-like in their pattern. It towered over me, and I sighed in relief when I noticed a small alcove formed in the base of the rocks. It was big enough that I could sit comfortably, and I plopped down, stretching my legs out in front of me as I prepared to wait.

I thought back to the loud blasts I'd heard from Oliver's end of the portal and truly contemplated if he had survived or not. If he was dead, and I was just sitting here like bait, then I might as well drown myself in the strange ocean now. It was probably Queen Tantaii, busting out from the rubble that had been dropped on her. I know they said Oliver was powerful, but was he powerful enough to go up against a faerie queen? I had my doubts. But what else could I do? I resolved to wait just for the night, and if he hadn't found me by morning then I'd venture out on my own. I needed food, and water. I was no use to anyone if I was dead.

My thoughts returned to Queen Tantaii. Formerly trapped queen of the Fae. *Mother*?

I frowned, my heartrate quickening as my emotions came rushing in, the information of what I had learned fully sinking in. I was half Fae, and my mother was the queen of the fucking Fae. It was hard to deny that she wasn't just an older, more ethereal version of my own reflection with how similar we looked. Same blonde hair, same big brown eyes. A normal person would probably be happy about that, but this was anything but normal.

What had she done that was so bad she was magically locked up for 500 years?

Olette. A version of myself that I'd chosen to forget. A version I didn't know. I couldn't imagine a world where I'd ever voluntarily give up my memories, not in a billion years. Memories were like my favorite trashy reality TV show—I needed them, no matter how embarrassing or cringe-worthy they might be.

And I needed them back now.

Where the hell is Oliver? The longer I sat there, the wider the pit of dread in my stomach grew. He should have been here by now.

"*Screeeee—*"

My head whipped up and I stared out of my alcove, cautiously moving into a kneeling position. I listened intently, until I heard the cry again. A high-pitched screech, but soft, like a baby animal.

"*Screeeeee!*"

It was louder this time, almost pained and I cautiously exited the cave. I followed the continuing cries, until I came up to a small rock ledge near the opposite side where a small figure tossed and turned.

I stared at the strange animal. It was unlike anything I'd ever seen before, like a cross between an eagle and a chicken. It was completely white, with feathered wings protruding from its torso and tucked tightly into its back. The only spot of color on it was its crimson eyes, currently scrunched in pain as it contorted on the ledge. A metal tipped arrow stuck out of its hind leg, and I softened in sympathy for the creature.

I approached the cheagle, careful to keep my hands out where it could see them. "Easy there, buddy. I'm just going to take a look and see if I can help you out, okay?"

Close enough now, I could see *it* was definitely a *he.* He focused one eye on me as he cried, his screams dying down into a soft mewling sound that made my heart wrench. I met his gaze, doing my best to give him a reassuring smile. He growled softly as I got closer, and when I reached one hand out to touch him, he swiped at me with his good leg, a deep slice opening on my hand.

"OW!" I shrieked, pulling my hand back and giving him the evil eye. "Do you want me to help you or not?" He quieted and regarded me, and for a split second I thought he almost looked human, but then he whimpered and pushed his injured leg out towards me.

"I don't think I should pull it out," I mused to myself. His leg was as white as the rest of him, stained with a shimmery liquid that oozed from the wound. *Silver blood?* "It's better to leave it in so you don't bleed out until we can—," What? Call for help? Get to a hospital? I had no way to help this creature.

The cheagle made a noise deep in his chest, and I squinted at him. He blinked at me expectantly and I shook my head, incredulous. "You want me to take this out?" He let out a soft chirp, sounding weak. This baby animal understood what I was saying. What kind of place was this?

I assessed the damage, becoming more hopeful as I looked on. The arrow was thinner than it had appeared, lightweight and tipped at both ends with a silvery grey metal which had gone straight through his thigh. Luckily the body of the arrow was wood, and the arrow was off to the side, hopefully missing any major arteries. If the animals in this realm even had arteries.

"This is going to hurt," I told him as I positioned my hands at one end of the arrow. A trickle of my blood dripped off my wrist, still leaking from the cut he'd made but already starting to itch, a sign my shifter healing was kicking in. I was relieved to know it still worked the same in this realm.

He closed his eyes, and I saw his sturdy chest expand as he took a deep breath. I didn't hesitate, gripping the arrow between my fists and wrenching my hands in different directions, breaking the arrow with only a little resistance. The cheagle shrieked in pain but I powered through, yanking both ends of the arrow out of their respective spots. His shriek intensified, before dying out into complete silence. I glanced at his prone form. He'd passed out from the pain, his chest still rising and falling steadily. *Poor baby.*

I stared at the wound, watching as the skin slowly started to knit itself back together. Now I understood why he'd wanted me to take it out, he healed just like I did. I stood there, not quite sure what to do with myself. I looked around in the blue haze of the landscape, no sign of any other life. Where had this little thing come from? And who had put this arrow in it?

It seemed to have gotten as dark as it was going to, the dual moons still casting enough light to be able to move around but not a good idea to travel in. The temperature had dropped, and I shivered lightly, missing my usual leather jacket. I eyed the creature, not wanting to leave him out here where he could be seen as easy prey to any passersby.

"You better not wake up and decide I'm the enemy," I muttered under my breath, gingerly cradling him in my arms and lifting him up. While I could probably take him, I didn't want to deal with those razor-sharp claws. He wasn't much bigger than a toddler, but he was dense, my arms dipping with the effort of carrying him. We retreated to my cave, and I gently laid him down in one corner, taking the opposite for myself. It was a tight squeeze, but he radiated a surprising amount of heat, and I found myself huddling closer to him. The wound on his leg was already healed, as was the cut on my hand, the dried crust of blood the only evidence of any injury at all.

I sat propped up with my back against the wall, doing my best to stay awake and stand guard until morning but exhaustion dragged at me, tugging at the corners of my resolve until I was a lost cause. Between the quiet peacefulness of the world outside, and the rhythmic breaths of the cheagle next to me, I faded into blissful oblivion.

Midnight Magic Preview
Chapter Two

It was the scream that woke me up.

At least, I thought it was a scream, until I opened my eyes and saw the baby cheagle, his little body practically vibrating with bristled energy, high pitched screeches coming from his maw. The wounded animal I had seen the night before was nowhere to be seen. My body seized in fear as I came face to face with what he was shrieking at.

A gargantuan creature blocked the entrance to our shelter. It stood a few heads taller than the cave mouth but had no trouble pinning me with its crimson stare. I couldn't see its wings, but the hulking shoulders told me everything I needed to know. This was not an animal to be fucked with. Its body was a mirror image of my unlikely companion, except where his feathers were white and pristine, this one's were in various hues of blue and green. Long, deadly claws adorned its feet, and I swallowed. Hard. I'd *definitely* die if grabbed by one of those. Its head dipped down toward me until we were level, before it opened its pointed beak, a sharp, menacing squawk bursting out.

This was mommy cheagle and she was *mad*.

I scrambled backward, my back thudding against the wall as I tried not to shit my pants in fear. Baby cheagle moved to stand in front of me, again screeching at its mother. Defending me, I realized. My heart would have warmed, if I wasn't a few feet away from my imminent death.

Mommy cheagle huffed as she angled her head downward, locking eyes with me.

'My kin tells me you helped him.' A gasp escaped me as she spoke into my mind. Her voice was surprisingly soft for how menacing she looked, yet strong and mature. There was a heaviness to her words, and it was almost too much for my mind to withstand, a dull ache setting in as I tried to adjust. It was nothing like when we had talked to each other in animal form back at the Clover pack. This was something different, something ancient. She waited for me to respond, but I just gaped my mouth open like a fish, struggling under the weight of her presence. *'You are not smart,'* she observed, her disdain blatant.

I cleared my throat, snapping my jaw shut and giving my head a quick shake. *Get your shit together.* "I didn't do much, just pulled the arrow out of his leg." The gratitude at my voice not wavering was immense. Defending my intelligence to this creature didn't seem like a smart move.

'He lives because of your actions. And for that, I owe you a debt.' Sunlight glinted off her scales, casting a crystalline glow throughout the cave. Her gaze was sincere, her head bowed, and the edges of my fear faded, replaced with a blanket of awe at the magnificent creature. *'That was an arrow forged by iron, which is toxic and deadly to most faerie kind. But if you ever lay a hand on another pagu, I will hook my talon in your throat, and eviscerate you.'* The terror flooded back, and I nodded in understanding. Pagu, not cheagle. No touchy. Got it.

'Come. Stop cowering on the ground.' I scooted out and up as she backed away from the entrance, still careful to keep a watchful eye in case I needed to run. It seemed like we had some weird sort of truce, but she'd also just threatened my life and I couldn't be too careful. Now on my feet, I could see she was easily a few feet taller than me. Her wings were pulled into her back, her

chest jutting forward proudly as she stood, eyeing my meager stature.

'I would have thought a princess would be more…impressive.' I tensed at her words, eyes wide.

"You know who I am?"

The beast snorted, light whisps of smoke escaping her. *'There are only three Fae that I know of with hair like that.'* I frowned at her, my hands coming up to smooth my golden tresses down. It'd been a while since I'd seen a brush, but I didn't think it was that bad. Then I thought back to the what I've seen. Cas, and Queen Tantaii, and their hair that mirrored my own.

"We are the only ones that have blonde hair?"

The pagu's eyes narrowed as she scanned me up and down critically. Judgment and anger lurked in their depth. I didn't know how, but she knew what I had done. She knew I'd forgotten. *'When you live as long as we do, knowledge is the universe's greatest gift. To squander that is a death sentence.'*

"I had a good reason." My response was defensive, but when being accused by a mythical flying creature, it was bound to happen. "You don't know what you're talking about." I cringed as soon as I said it. Not only would upsetting this creature likely get me killed, but *I* didn't even know what I was talking about. I was still trying to wrap my head around how my past self could have made such a decision. Probably the same way I always made decisions. *Without thinking first.*

She snorted, shuffling restlessly where she stood. *'Why are you here?'*

"Well . . . It all started when I was kidnapped by a rude ass cu—"

'I do not care, halfling. Why are you sleeping on this beach? This is pagu territory. I would normally skin any trespassers who dare to enter and feed their flesh to my children.'

My breathing wavered but I steeled myself, doing my best to remind myself that if she wanted to kill me, she would have by now. *Just keep telling yourself that.* "I'm looking for my companion. We were separated when he opened a portal for me to this realm, but he was attacked before he could follow me through."

I looked out toward the sea, the sun sitting low on the horizon as it rose, casting a brilliant golden pathway across the water's surface. Its shimmer combined with the red of the water made it look like a thousand tiny flames dancing, painting the sea in an impressive display of fiery hues that stretched on forever.

"I was hoping he'd show up by morning." My words were soft, resigned to what had probably happened. Oliver hadn't made it, and now I was stuck here alone. Panic started to seep in, weaving its way around my fragile walls like a serpent coiling to strike.

'I will help you, and the debt will be paid.' I thought about refusing, still not entirely sure this animal didn't still want to kill me. But what other choice did I have? I needed to find Oliver. I needed food, water, and shelter. I needed her help.

"Thank you. Do you have a name? What can I call you? I'm Rowan."

'The closest translation to your language would be Aura. He has not earned his name yet.' She turned to the baby, who had been watching us silently for the past few minutes. After a few seconds of chattering between the two that sounded suspiciously like an argument, he approached me, coming to a stop before me. He stared at me expectantly, his red eyes looking as innocent as possible, and I chided myself for being afraid of the small animal.

I stooped down, closer to his height, and craned my neck toward him, not sure what he wanted but he'd also saved me from getting eaten, so a little trust was warranted. He lightly laid his beak on my arm, meeting my eyes, and I melted. He was thanking me. "You're welcome little dude." I said, as I cautiously reached out, giving his head a small pat.

'Go back to the stronghold," Aura glared at him until he hunched his shoulders for a moment before his wings shot out, and he launched himself into the air unsteadily. With a few surges, he was airborne, flying off into the distance, wavering slightly back

and forth in the air as he went, until he was just a small speck in the distance.

'Let us go, I believe I know where your friend is. If I am right, we need to get there sooner than later. Normally I would only let my marked rider on my back, but I will make an exception this time.'

"Did you just say *rider*?"

The rocky terrain underneath us shifted slightly as Aura bent down, her legs folding underneath themselves until she resembled a chicken sitting on her eggs. Except there was no eggs, only a very pointed look she was giving me that I really didn't want to see.

'Get on. Try anything funny and I'll slit your throat.'

Afterword

If you read this far, holy crap, thank you.

I was elbows deep in another project when Rowan came barging into my head, demanding I tell her story. I tried to ignore her, but, as I'm sure you've noticed, she doesn't take no for an answer. I put everything on the backburner for her, and I am so grateful that I did. Creating and sharing her world with you was an absolute honor.

I've spent a lot of my life not finishing things, and the fact that I wrote a whole ass book is mind-boggling to me. I hope you ha as much fun reading this as I did writing it. I can't wait to continue telling my stories, and I will continue to do so far as long as you are willing to read them.

Love always,
Sav

About the Author

Savannah is a California native and Las Vegas dweller. She was that kid that went to class with a stack full of books and paid absolutely no attention to the teacher. After reading her way through the library and not seeing the stories she wanted, she decided to write her own!

Savannah Lee writes 18+ mature urban fantasy and paranormal romance stories.

Join my Facebook group!
Savannah Lee's Silly Rabbits

Instagram
@savannahleeauthor

TikTok
@savannahleewrites

Goodreads
https://www.goodreads.com/author/show/6540743.Savannah_Lee

Follow me on Amazon!
https://www.amazon.com/stores/Savannah-Lee/author/B0C4KK3954

Also by Savannah Lee

CLOVER PACK SERIES

Midnight Mated #1

Midnight Magic #2

Midnight Mayhem #3

Made in the USA
Monee, IL
02 December 2023